# ETHAN

PREQUEL
NOVELLA

*NEW YORK TIMES* BESTSELLING AUTHOR
# P.T. MICHELLE

# ETHAN

SERIES READING ORDER

**Brightest Kind of Darkness Series**

ETHAN *
BRIGHTEST KIND OF DARKNESS
LUCID
DESTINY
DESIRE
AWAKEN

*ETHAN is a prequel that delves deeper into Ethan's background. It's best read **after** BRIGHTEST KIND OF DARKNESS.

The Brightest Kind of Darkness series is best suited for readers 16+.

# CHAPTER 1

*H*eavy claws clamp on to my arms, grabbing me from behind.

*A piercing screech reverberates to the back of my skull.*

*In the dim light, I can make out scales and long teeth, but it's the putrid smell that twists my stomach in knots.*

*The creature's powerful nails dig into the muscles of my forearms, latching on. I shudder as darkness engulfs me like a lead cape, weighing me down, always trying to pull me under.*

*Somewhere in the recesses of my mind, a whisper trickles through.* Don't you feel the welcome of eternal bliss? No more seeing. No more feeling. Just close your eyes and sleep.

*Primeval survival erupts from deep within me, and I tug hard, gritting my teeth through the nails slicing along my arms like knives sliding through butter. Pain is my constant companion here. It's one thing I can count on.*

*Pressure clamps my chest and fire licks my skin, but I let out a surprisingly inhuman growl and pivot, plowing a fist into the creature's snout. The moment his hold loosens, I break free.*

I awake on a gulp of air and yank upright in a tangle of

bed sheets. My dreams seem to be getting worse. I quickly run my fingers across the tattoo on my forearm and blow out a harsh breath. *Still intact.* Sweat trickles down my neck and chest as I roll my head from one shoulder to the other and mutter, "Just another messed up night."

Scrubbing my disheveled hair from my face, I lean over and reach for my sketchpad and pencil from the carpet, but my hands are shaking too much to draw a straight line. I grunt and set them aside for later. It's not like the image will fade like normal dreams do. These images are seared in my memory with laser precision.

The bottle of pills on my nightstand mocks me, so I carry it into the bathroom and run the sink's tap. "Go ahead," a gravelly voice from my dream grates in my ear. "Try to put a muzzle on me." I wait several seconds, then pull out a pill. When a sneering snarl reverberates in my head, I narrow my gaze and promptly drop it in the toilet. After I flush, I ignore my downturned lips in the mirror. Instead, I focus on the flicker of amusement in the deep blue eyes peering through my dark bangs. The voice is gone. For now.

You know you're a hundred-and-eighty degrees of effed up when you give *yourself* a disapproving frown. Then again, the fact I know what I'm doing should qualify as sane behavior. Conscious disregard works for me. I refuse to experience life cocooned in a layer of hazy, mind-numbing reality. I kind of like to give a damn.

"Great birthday so far," I snark at my reflection before turning on the shower.

"HAPPY SEVENTEENTH, BRO." Samson's blond eyebrows elevate from behind his morning cup of coffee as he zings a familiar blue plastic bag from my favorite electronics store across the kitchen table toward me.

I catch the bag just before it slides off onto the floor. Maybe he got me those headphones I've been wanting.

Samson chuckles and takes a sip while I pull out my present. He's watching me warily, like I'm some kind of science experiment.

"Thanks," I mutter unenthusiastically and set the unopened cell phone box on the counter, then turn to the fridge.

"Ethan…" my brother begins on a heavy sigh.

"I don't need a phone," I say and reach for the orange juice.

"You're starting at the new school tomorrow. I'd like this time to go better."

The disappointment in his voice tightens my grip on the door handle. "I'll be fine."

"Getting kicked out of your last school is not fine. You need to find a way to redirect yourself positively. I just want to know—"

"Where I *am* at all times." Swiping up the juice box, I lean on the fridge door and stare at the wall, reliving the moment when the police found me at my secret hang-out spot and put me in cuffs. I got hauled away to jail, all because my parents believed I was the one who broke into our lake house and vandalized my dad's BMW. In my parents' minds, only drugs could explain my sudden erratic behavior. I learned two lessons that day: never to trust my parents, and there's a downside to hanging with people *with* drug habits. "You going to use it to have me arrested too?"

"Don't compare me to them. Ever," my brother grates, then softens his tone. "I'm not trying to keep tabs on you,

Ethan. I'll just feel better knowing you can call me if...you need anything."

*So you can talk me out of going off the rails like I did at my last school?* I lift the juice box to my lips and gulp down several noisy swallows.

"Are you trying to piss me off?"

*Maybe. Probably.* He hates when I don't use a cup. "No." Normally he has already left for work by now. I know he stayed to wish me a happy birthday. I set the juice back on the rack and shut the door, intending to let it go when my gaze snags on the blue envelope on the table that wasn't there a second ago.

"Found that in the mailbox this morning," he says quietly, folding his arms across his dress shirt. "They'll call sometime today."

*No they won't.*

Samson tries to look casual, yet slight hope and sympathy lurks as his light blue gaze pings between the envelope and me. Samson might be five years older, but he gets me, even if he doesn't understand what I really deal with. He accepts without judgement, which I appreciate, but I don't want his sympathy.

I stare at the card. *Ethan Harris* is stamped on the address label. The return address label reads *Sherri and Gerald Harris.* Labels. I'm now a name on their obligatory card list along with the rest of their country club friends. *Nice.* I snatch up the card and head back toward my room.

"Aren't you going to open it?"

"You're going to be late for work if you don't leave now," I call over my shoulder.

I WAIT until Samson's car pulls out of the driveway, then grab my mp3 player and car keys and lock up the house. Oak Lawn Cemetery is quiet when I pull up. It's so early no one's out. Not even the old caretaker I've seen shuffling around from time to time. Suits me fine. I'm not in the mood for idle chitchat.

The main gate is locked, so I skirt the fence surrounding the large cemetery until I see the willow at the back of the property. It takes me all of two seconds to climb the thick wrought iron that's apparently there for ornamental purposes. It's not like people go around breaking into cemeteries.

The trees sport various shades of oranges, reds, and yellows, but my gaze tracks the ravens scattered throughout their limbs. The birds emit guttural greetings. I nod to them, but keep my head down as I head toward the willow.

I figure everyone has a place they go. The willow is my place. I lean against its thick trunk and let its weeping branches wrap me in a feeling of seclusion. In a few weeks the fronds will drop and I'll be visible among the grove of trees lining the back of the cemetery, but until then it's my own personal haven. I found this space not long after I moved to Virginia with my brother. Samson's the strong silent type, saying as little as possible. Sometimes I like that about him. The less probing questions the better. But other times, when I'm feeling overwhelmed by all the noise going on in my head, all the images and voices that refuse to give me peace, I wish he'd push for answers. Demand them even. For now… the willow suffices.

With a sigh I plug in my earbuds and turn on a Southern rock tune, then reach inside my jacket and remove the card from my parents. I dig its sharp corners into the pads of my fingers and wait, savoring the tiny spark of hope. For a few brief moments I fantasize about the huge sweeping apology poured into a long, drawn out letter full of love and acceptance.

I tear into the envelope and stare at the generic it-could've-been-anyone's-birthday card greeting. HAPPY BIRTHDAY it reads in bold blue letters on a plain bright yellow background. I wish they weren't, but my hands shake as I flip it open.

**Here's hoping you have a great birthday.**

*Mom and Dad*

They didn't even bother putting my name in front of the printed birthday wish that comes standard on the card. Out of morbid curiosity, I glance at the check tucked in the crease. Ten thousand dollars. *For your college fund* the bank had typed in the memo section. Guess the price of guilt has gone up. Last year's check was five grand.

My attention slides to the *Mom and Dad* signature. It's my mom's handwriting. Maybe next year the signature will be a rubber stamp like they use on their Christmas cards that says, *Much love, Sherri and Gerald.* Somehow that might sound more sincere.

Next year, I won't even open it.

Sliding the check and card back into the envelope, I clench my jaw and pull a lighter from my pocket. I sit up straighter to quash the twist in my stomach as the blue envelope bursts into flames. Before the licking heat reaches my fingers, I drop the flaming paper in the spot scorched by my past birthday and Christmas cards. Over in a disappointing flash. Just like this birthday. Right before the last of the flames die, I close my eyes and pretend I'm blowing it out. *I want to be a normal seventeen-year-old, who focuses on sports and girls and where I'm going to college. But I'd settle for never hearing another taunting voice or seeing another dark, horrifying image in my mind or my dreams ever again.*

Exhaling a resigned sigh, I open my eyes and move to switch my current song to something more in tune with my sour mood when a strange noise bleeds through. *What is that?* I pause the music and pull out my earbuds to listen. A second or two later a pitiful sound carries on the fall wind whipping through the oaks in the cemetery. Someone is crying.

I lean against the tree and squeeze my eyes closed, trying to shut it out. This is a cemetery, after all. It's likely anyone who's here is crying for a reason that's beyond fixable. But the wails are so utterly helpless and heartfelt, I'm on my feet and weaving past mausoleums and rows of headstones before I realize it.

I reach a low headstone and frown. The bawling is clearly coming from this direction, but I don't see anyone. Then I round the side of the headstone and the sight of a small boy curled up on his side in front of the stone knocks the self-pity wind right out of me. He's clutching a lone flower in his hand; probably picked it from someone's garden on his way here.

"Hey," I say, squatting next to him.

He quickly gulps and sits up, eyes wide. Scrubbing the tear tracks from his dark cheeks, he says, "Who are you? You're not supposed to be here!"

He's so adamant, my eyebrows elevate. "I'm not?"

The kid shakes his head and runs his free hand along his nearly shaved scalp. A pink scar above his left ear stands out against his dark hair and skin underneath. "Nah, no one's here this early. Even Mr. Thomas."

*So that's the old caretaker's name.* I tilt my head and give a brief smile. "You want to cry in peace?"

7

He starts to nod, then scowls. "I wasn't crying. I'm not a baby!"

I touch the headstone he's leaning against and peer around him to read the inscription. "Is this someone you knew?"

Sadness falls over his face as he sets the flower against the stone, then pulls a toy car out of his coat pocket. Running it along his leg, he mumbles, "My mom died when I was six."

The way he holds on to that car tells me it's more than just a toy to him. "And how old are you now?"

His cheeks puff with pride. "I'm six and a half."

"That half a year makes all the difference," I say, nodding sagely. "I'm Ethan. What's your name?"

He scrunches his nose in doubt. "I'm not supposed to talk to strangers."

I shrug and sit down. "Okay, I'll just call you Todd then."

"That's not my name," he says, jerking upright. "I'm Marcus."

"Nice to meet you, Marcus." I incline my head toward the headstone. "I take it you're here to talk to your mom. I'm sorry she's not able to reply, but if you want, I'll be happy to be your sounding board."

"Huh? Sounding what?"

I chuckle. "Someone to talk to about whatever's bothering you."

"Aren't you supposed to be in school?" he accuses as he slides the car's wheels along the side of his squeaky-clean tennis shoes. Must've just gotten them.

"Aren't you?"

He smiles at that, flashing small perfect teeth as he sets the car down and picks up a stick. "Yeah, but I had a bad morning, so I gave myself a day off."

8

I eye him. Sounds like something he's heard an adult say before. "You think your teachers will feel that way?"

A crease forms between his eyebrows. "Prolly not."

"Tell me about your bad morning. I know a thing or two about those." *I'm the King of Understatement.*

He shrugs and digs at the ground with the stick. Just as I start to say something else, he drops the stick and grabs on to the Velcro strap on his shoe. Ripping it open violently, he grumbles, "My dad says I'm a baby because I don't know how to tie my shoes yet."

*Is that all?* I want to sputter, but as I watch him refasten the Velcro strap, a horrific smell floats my way. *I can't believe that putrid stench is following me from my dreams now.* Images and voices I'm learning to deal with but smells are new, making it feel more real somehow. *Well, shit. Probably should've taken the damn pill.* The stench grows stronger with the boy's jerky movements, drawing my gaze to his wrist. Where his jacket has ridden up, deep bruises in various shades—bruises on top of bruises—show in vivid clarity against his darker skin tone.

Someone has grabbed him hard and repeatedly. I look into his eyes and recognize his haunted, trapped expression. My circumstances are entirely different, but I get the feeling of never being able to escape.

I can touch his shoulder and console him, but comfort is fleeting; it means you depended on someone else to get you through. I've learned that pain, both emotional and physical, can be a necessary evil, a visceral reminder life is gritty and real. When you finally stumble your way through the discomfort, you learn from it. Coping tools are better. They teach you how to survive.

So, tools it is. I untie the shoelace on one of my Chucks. "Want to see how I tie my shoes?" I say as I make two loops, one on each lace. I twist the two loops together then flip one of the loops around the other, tying them together. As I finish with a double knot, the boy snickers.

"That's a weird way of tying shoes."

I glance at him through my bangs, eyebrows raised. "Says the kid who can't tie his own shoes." Marcus frowns and starts to turn away, but I continue, "This is called the bunny-ears method. I learned it in kindergarten and to this day people still laugh at me when they see me tie my shoes."

"Then why don't you learn the other way?"

I shrug. "Why? This way works. It's what I know. Sometimes you have to stand up for yourself, Marcus, even if the way you choose to do things is different from everyone else. It doesn't make you any less. It just makes you unique. Never compromise your exceptionalness."

"Exceptional-ness?" His brow creases as he stumbles through the word. "Is that a real word?"

I hold his skeptical gaze. "Today it is."

Marcus presses his lips and appears to mull over my comment. Gesturing to my shoe, he says, "Can you show me again?"

After I show him once more, I let Marcus practice on my shoe until he can do it himself.

I pull out a candy bar I brought to "celebrate" my annual card burning. As I tear open the wrapping, I ask, "You want to split this with me?"

Marcus nods vigorously.

While we enjoy the chocolate, nuts, and caramel goodness, a quiet descends between us. The ravens' soft croaks and rack sounds start up, growing louder as if they're trying to outdo one another. Marcus slides an apprehensive glance toward the trees. "I've never seen so many of these birds here before."

"Really?" I say in surprise, following his gaze. "Must be

the time of day you come. There's always a whole horde whenever I'm here."

A slight shudder ripples through the little boy. "You don't think they're kind of creepy?"

I laugh. I can't help it. I've never been bothered by ravens. Everywhere we've lived, they've been around. Unlike hummingbirds in the spring, finches in the summer, and geese in the fall, ravens claim *all* the seasons. "You should look ravens up some time. They're actually pretty smart birds, despite the fact they eat carrion. The next time you come for a visit, think of them as constant companions and you'll never feel alone again."

Marcus ponders for a few seconds as he licks the chocolate off his fingers. Tilting his head, he asks, "What if the ravens don't help?"

"Tell you what, if you ever need to talk," I pause and nod toward the toy car he'd tucked back in his pocket, "then leave your car on top of your mother's grave. I'll show up this time the next day. Sound good?"

He presses his lips together, then nods. "I'll leave another car, but not this one. My mom gave it to me right before she died."

He tries to look tough, but I can tell he's trying hard not to cry. Sometimes, even armed with tools, everyone needs a little comfort. I smile and hold out my hand. "It's a deal. Let's shake on it."

# CHAPTER 2

*A*fternoon sun shines down on me as I leave the cemetery, making me tense and antsy. My day's half gone. Tomorrow I'll start at the new school, Blue Ridge, so I need to make the most of my last day of the "freedom" Central gave me a week ago.

Thoughts about my last school brought the ragtag group I hung with to mind. *How are the guys doing since I left a week ago?* There's Blade (for his skill with a switchblade), Creeper (for his harmless ability to mentally undress girls in various ways), Mo (for his spiked Mohawk), and lastly Shaun rounds out the group. They all go by nicknames, except Shaun. Actually, he does too, since half the time the guys call him Dead, which is short for *Shaun of the Dead*. Out of the four of them, Shaun is probably the most normal. Well, if you call a group of total screw-ups normal. Maybe it's a "misery loves company" kind of thing, but however it happened, these guys gravitated toward each other like flies to the steaming pile of crap they called their home lives. And so they made the perfect group for me to start hanging with at Central high school.

Knowing the guys the way I do, now that I'm not there to glue them together, at least one has skipped school part of the week, another is spending his days in in-school suspension, and the other two are looking for ways to get in trouble. Before I got kicked out of Central last week, we mostly spent the afternoons hanging in the school parking lot at the end of the day talking about cars and music. The memory of Shaun slapping Creeper on the shoulder last Tuesday has me turning toward the downtown mall. He'd looked at me and said, "Since you like that Southern rock shit, you should check out the Irish pub McCormicks downtown. We go there when we ditch, and every once in a while, the drummer let's Creeps here jump in and practice with the house band Waylaid."

It's a pain to make up work at school if I miss, so today might be my only chance to hear this band Shaun mentioned. I'm always looking for new music to add to my collection. I park my car in the parking deck and make my way a few streets over to the brickyard mall. My pace picks up as that grating voice starts creeping in my head once more. *You really don't think music will help, do you? You can never get away from me. I'm always here. In your dreams. In your head. F-o-r-e-v-e-r.*

The back of my head twinges and I feel an image trying to come through. I shake my head and start running, hoping to keep it from invading my sight, but an image floats in my vision regardless.

I halt so I don't unintentionally run into a building or pole and squeeze my eyes shut. Grotesque skeletal hands with half sloughed-off flesh and long, dirty nails are reaching for my throat. I grit my teeth and try to clear my mind while mentally chanting, *It's not real. It's not real.* Over and over.

A bell pings right before someone zooms by. The jarring

sound obliterates the image and my eyes fly open in time to see an old woman riding a bike, complete with a basket full of groceries in the front of the old-style handlebars.

Thankful to be jerked back to reality, I quickly scan for the pub. When my gaze locks on the big M stamped on the shamrock sign nestled in the far corner of the mall, a half smile tugs my lips as Shaun's last comment about the place comes back to me. "Check McCormicks out. Later we'll come with. We've been banned for a while due to my fist shaking hands with some asshole's face." I scrub my overnight beard, glad I'd skipped shaving this morning. I look more like my fake ID this way.

McCormicks is just like any other pub, yet it still has its own homey feel with a heavy mahogany bar that spans an entire wall and locals' beer steins hanging down from the overhead hooks surrounding the bar. The place is dimly lit and cozy despite the large amount of seating that reaches far back from the corner stage. I instantly feel at home the moment I walk in and see the placard touting the house band's name, Weylaid spelled with an 'e'. There has to be a story behind that.

The band of three is preparing to warm up. I weave my way through the tables and take a seat at a round two-person table in the middle of the room. An older guy with short gray hair sits at a table against the wall eating a sandwich and nursing his beer, while two women occupy the table closest to the stage. Every so often they try to talk to one of the band members, but he's too busy on his phone to pay them any attention.

The all-business looking dark-haired guy, who obviously leads the band, is talking on his phone. "Duke, where are you, man? We need to get this new song down before the weekend. You helped write the damned thing, so get your groupie-loving ass down here!"

As the guy smiles and mouths "not you" at the two girls sitting near the stage, a sleepy bartender with red dreads stops at my table and asks in a heavy Irish accent, "ID please."

I hand him my card and say, "I'll just have a Coke."

He tosses my ID on the table and heads off, while I turn my attention back to the band.

The bald drummer raises a pierced eyebrow, then spins a drumstick around one hand. "He was out with Miranda last night. We won't see him 'til two hours before show time."

"Why the hell didn't you tell me before now?"

The drummer shrugs. "You were too busy being a prima donna—"

"Fuck you, Ivan."

Ivan blows him a kiss and laughs. "Best offer I've had all week. Oooh, I know, Dom, why don't you ask if anyone out there can fill in for our missing bassist."

Dom scowls at him and makes a rude gesture. The quiet blond guy behind him snickers as he tunes his guitar. I can't help but smile. These guys act like the guys from my old school. No wonder Shaun and Creeper like watching them warm up.

"Then I will." Ivan stands behind his drum set and cups his hands over his eyes to block out the spotlights. "Anyone out there know how to play the bass geetar?"

I snort at his utter smartassness, then frown when the guy named Dom stands and points to the middle of the room. "You know how to play?"

*Who's he talking to?* I start to glance behind me, then realize my arm is raised. I slowly lower my hand as my stomach drops. What is wrong with me? I don't know jack about playing the guitar.

"Well, do you?" Ivan asks. Turning, he pulls out a bass guitar from a case against the wall and holds it up. "You can borrow this one."

I've lost the ability to speak, and while "this is total bull-shit" rambles inside my head, my feet pull me toward the stage in the corner of the room. Once I step on the stage, I honestly start to believe I have completely lost my mind, but then my hand clasps the guitar's neck and the feel of the strings under my fingers settles my pounding heart with old familiarity.

"I do," I murmur and sit down on the stool the other guitar player slides toward me with his foot. The second I settle the instrument on my thigh, I close my eyes and begin plucking and tuning until it sounds right.

Dom picks up his guitar and tries to hand me sheet music, but I shake my head and ask them to play a song. Once I hear it, I jump in and improvise, while Dom sings and plays lead, and the blond guy I heard them call Chance plays rhythm. Then the real jamming begins.

I play anything and everything they throw my way. The band's music easily moves from rock and Southern rock songs in the vein of The Black Crowes' "Hard to Handle" and "She Talks to Angels" to power ballads that remind me of Parachute's "Forever and Always" and "Kiss Me Slowly."

I really like the way they mix it up, and the amazing thing is, while I'm engrossed in the songs…nothing is going on in my head but the music. There's no room for screaming, no space for thoughts about my dreams or freaky images. It's like the process of creating music overlays the quagmire, muffling all my worries to the size of a gnat flitting at a distance, still there but barely noticeable.

Duke finally arrives, his longish, auburn hair surfer messy. When the two girls make swoony sounds as he swaggers past them with a cocky grin, Dom's earlier "groupie-loving" comment seems appropriate.

Duke presses his mouth when he looks my way, apparently not thrilled I'm playing the bass parts. The band members tell him to get the hell over himself and join in. He grudgingly sits down with another guitar and we play a couple of tunes together. As I slide off the stool, Duke shoves his hand toward me. "Great playing with you…" He pauses and raises an eyebrow.

"Add." I shake his hand in a firm grip, wondering why the name Add had slipped out instead of my real name.

"Like one-plus-one?" Ivan looks amused, then shakes his head. "Nah, we'll just call you Adder."

Instead of being offended that he'd renamed me after a snake, an ache briefly twists in my heart. Confused by the whole scenario, I look back at Duke, who smiles and shakes his head like they've just shared an inside joke. "May as well get used to it."

While I lean over to set the guitar back in its case, Ivan nods to my arm. "Nice dragon." He shoves his sleeve up to show me the ink at the top of his right bicep. It's some kind of Asian symbol. "Means persevere." Respect flickers in his dark eyes as they slide back to my forearm. "That had to have taken a while. Must have a high pain tolerance."

I glance down at the dragon on my arm and give a self-deprecating smile. "You could say that."

Dom claps me on the shoulder before I leave. "Thanks for playing with us. We're happy to have you join us anytime, Adder," he finishes, sliding a grin to Ivan.

I nod and address the four of them, "Where'd Weylaid come from anyway?"

Dom laughs. "Wey is Duke's real name. He threw out the

name Weylaid for the band name and we thought it was funny."

I raise my eyebrow. *Duke's a stage name? I don't feel so bad about lying now.*

Ivan rolls his eyes. "It's about how music hijacks your life, man, but sex sells so we kept it." With a wide grin, he pushes back his leather vest for me to read his t-shirt underneath. ***Have you been* Weylaid? *Once will never be enough!*** "Let me know if you want one. I can hook you up."

Duke snorts and jerks his head toward Ivan. "Iv's our marketing spin doctor. How do you think I ended up with the name Duke?"

More than likely Chance's name is made up too. I probably *don't* want to know how Dom ended up with his name if Ivan dubbed it. Chuckling, I turn to leave.

After such a surreal experience, joy and disbelief swing wildly through me, but as I walk out of the bar a cold sweat breaks out on my body and my hands start to shake. Now that my mind isn't consumed by the music, questions boomerang inside my head. *How did I know how to do that?* It's like my body knew what my mind didn't and acted on instinct. As much as the past several hours of playing music had improved my mood, it also brought on a different kind of anxiety I've never experienced before. Guilt.

Heading for the parking deck, I frown as I turn down the alley that'll save me walking time. *How can I revel in this amazing day when this talent isn't mine?* It's like enjoying the exhilarating feeling of finally learning to ride a bike while skipping the scrapes and bruises stage. It feels like cheating. Same as going by Adder instead of Ethan. It's all bullshit…and I don't trust it, which is why I'll never go back to McCormicks.

Decision made, I slide into my car and pull out of the deck. But as I turn onto the highway, I can't seem to get what just happened out of my mind. Confusion tightens my hands on the steering wheel, turning my knuckles as white as the moon lighting my path home. I can't believe I'm right back where I started this morning, anxious and full of doubt. I glance up at the full moon with a wry twist of my lips. The paper mentioned that a lunar eclipse is supposed to occur in the early morning hours tonight. Why do any "feel good" moments I have seem as rare and fleeting as that impending celestial event? Setting my jaw, I screech around the corner into the entrance of my neighborhood.

Just as I pull into our driveway, my headlights shine on Shaun's wavy brown hair. *What's he doing here?* He turns and ambles off my porch toward my car as I cut the engine.

Shutting the car door, I turn his way and a fist jams into my shoulder, knocking me back. "We miss your intense ass," he says with a grin. "How's life on the outside?"

I rub my sore shoulder and smirk. I think of school as a kind of "jail" too, but for an entirely different reason. "I've only been gone a week."

Shaun scrubs his messy hair and frowns. "It didn't take long for things to go to shit once you left, though."

I don't know what to say. I'm out of their lives now, so I shove my hands in my jeans pockets, lean back against my car and change the subject. "How'd you know where I live?"

Shaun flips his dark hood back up over his head—the mode I'm used to seeing him in—and adopts a mischievous grin as he taps his temple. "Creeper distracted the secretary by flipping out about the 'unfair and egregious'—can you believe he pulled that word out his ass?—detention his teacher had given him. While 'old gray hair' wasn't looking, I hopped on the school's computer and looked you up."

I cross my arms and stiffen. "Why?"

"Did you really think we'd let it pass, Harris?" Shaun

pulls off his backpack and unzips it.

My brows drop into a deep vee. "Let what pass?"

Shaun yanks a plastic bag out of his backpack and throws it at me. "Happy birthday, you suspicious bastard."

I catch the gift with my chest and cough before the box falls into my hands. I'm so surprised my hands tremble a little as I withdraw the headphones box from the bag. "These are expensive, Shaun." I meet his gaze, my own slightly narrow. "How'd you pay for them?"

"What?" Shaun scowls and jerks his backpack onto his shoulders once more. "I don't look like I can afford two-hundred-dollar headphones?"

I slide the gift back into the bag, my lips twitching. "Yeah, possibly for yourself, but not for someone you barely know."

"And whose fault is that, Ethan, huh?" Shaun's face is strained, the grooves around his mouth more pronounced than I've seen since I first met him. Has his dad lost his job again? Has his mom finally left like she's been threatening to do if that happened? "You barely tell us about yourself, yet you somehow manage to ferret out all our dirty secrets. I still want to know which of the douchebags spilled the beans about my shithole life."

He's clenching his teeth, working himself up, so I grip his shoulder and squeeze. "Does it really matter? Thanks for remembering my birthday and for the gift. It means a lot."

Shaun dips his head and takes a couple of deep breaths, then meets my gaze. "You're welcome. We all pitched in." He digs his hands deep into his hoodie pockets. "Came up a little short, but I left an IOU in the envelope of money at the register where they'll find it."

I snort to keep from laughing. This is total Shaun. He tries to do the right thing, but does it by skating a very gray line. "Um, how much short?"

21

A sheepish look crosses his face. "Just twenty."

I release his shoulder and shake my head, smiling. "Well, it's the thought that counts. Thanks for making my birthday not totally suck."

Shaun flashes a wide grin. "You're welcome. And just 'cause we don't go to the same school anymore doesn't mean we can't hang. That's what friends do, you know. We're there for each other."

Friends? I straighten and try not to let the apprehension show on my face. People say they want to know about you, but when the truth comes out, they suddenly can't meet your gaze. If your own parents can't deal, how can you expect friends to? Sharing is never a good idea. The less these guys know about me, the better.

Shaun nods to the bag and starts to back down my driveway. "I wrote my number on a piece of paper and threw it in there with your gift. Call me sometime."

I frown after him. He told me he lives in Arbor Creek apartments, which is a good five miles from my house. "You want a lift home?"

"Nah, I like walking." He shrugs and taps his temple. "Clears the head."

I watch Shaun walk away and try to ignore the twinge of worry in my chest. He said he sold his car because the upkeep costs too much. I know the real reason he walks everywhere, though. Six months ago his dad sold his car to pay bills after he lost his last job. The shitty part is that Shaun had worked three jobs to buy the car himself. It might've been a clunker, but it was *his* POS. When he tried to confront his dad, he ended up a punching bag for his efforts.

Even though my baggage isn't anything like normal people's crap, in some ways, my life is easier. At least I tell myself that as I unlock the front door. The house is quiet. Samson won't be home for another hour.

An envelope sits on the table in the kitchen with *Happy Birthday!* written on the outside. I stare at it for at least a minute before I tear along the flap.

As I flip open the card, a receipt from a local electronics store falls into my hand. It's for car speakers.

*Forget the phone. Just know I'm here for you. New beginnings need a path. Let the music lead you down the right road, little brother. The speakers are in the garage.*

*Samson*

My lungs constrict then expand with gratitude. Even though he can't possibly have known what I've been doing for half the day, my brother has developed this knack for knowing what I need. Just like he did two years ago, and then again when I turned sixteen. I stare at the receipt as memories of my sixteenth birthday rush forth, bringing with them a deluge of conflicted emotions.

*The moment I walked in the door late from school, Samson heaved a sigh while sifting through the mail at the kitchen table. "Bad day?"*

*Shrugging, I grabbed the loaf of bread, then retrieved the jar of peanut butter from the cabinet. "Seems to be the way the year's going."*

*Samson tore a piece of junk mail in half and tossed it in the trash pile. "Detention shouldn't go so late, Ethan."*

*I lifted my shoulders and continued spreading peanut butter on the bread. "I tried to tell Mr. Phillips that. He didn't see it that way."*

*My brother picked up another piece of mail and gestured to the pile with the envelope. "I'm sure you've got a card in here somewhere. Just haven't gotten through it yet."*

*"Not holding my breath," I mumbled around a bite of bread. We'd played this game for four weeks now. How much longer would my brother continue this charade?*

*Samson rolled his eyes and quickly thumbed through the mail to prove me wrong. As he slowed down toward the end of the stack, I tried not to let it show how much it bothered me that our parents had forgotten my birthday. My sixteenth, no less. Then again, maybe it's their way of punishing me for leaving. I straightened my spine and jammed the last bite of sandwich in my mouth. I told myself I didn't give a damn that they haven't called to ask me to come home; the same thought I've had every day since I left.*

*Grabbing his keys, Samson stood and said in a gruff voice, "Let's go."*

*"Where are we going?"*

*"You'll see when we get there," he called over his shoulder, heading for the door.*

*I glanced sideways as my brother pulled into Mike's Body Shop. "Why'd you bring me here? You want me to learn to be a mechanic?"*

*Samson snorted. "Mike's got that part taken care of."*

*"Then why——"*

*"Just get out of the car and follow me."*

*I grudgingly followed my brother to the back of the main garage, hands tucked in my jeans pockets, sweatshirt hood pulled up over my head.*

*We stopped at the back door and Samson rang the doorbell. My brother glanced my way and grunted in annoyance. Right before the door opened he yanked my hood off. I frowned, but left it down. He was acting so weird.*

*Mike's gray head popped out and he said in a scratchy voice, "Been waiting for you."*

*"Evening, Mike," Samson smiled and rocked back on his heels.*

*The mechanic flashed a grin, then handed my brother an envelope. "I'll leave you to it."*

*When Mike shut the door in our faces, I turned a "that dude's strange" gaze my brother's way, but the main garage door started to rise, distracting me.*

*As soon as the door was halfway up, Samson pulled me under it.*

*Nodding toward the black car in the center of the garage bay, he said, "It needs some work, but Mike says he'll be happy to teach you. I know how much you like vintage, so I thought you'd appreciate working on it. Happy birthday, little brother."*

*I gaped at the 1969 Mustang, then pulled my gaze back to Samson. "It's mine?"*

*Eyes gleaming, he pushed me forward. "How else are you going to get to school? The bus sucks."*

*Lifting my hand toward the car, I said, "But that's too much."*

*Samson clamped his hand on my shoulder and squeezed. "I can't undo our parents' stupidity, Ethan. God knows I wish I could." He nodded toward the car. "I'd like you to think of this as a new beginning."*

*His comment knocked me in the gut. He was saying my life with him was permanent, that hoping our parents will eventually beg me to come home was fruitless. I closed my eyes and swallowed several times before I accepted my new reality and the new date for my birthday. From here on out, I would always think of my birthday as October 24th, the day I got my car. I met my brother's expectant blue gaze. "You didn't have to get me a car for my birth—"*

*"Shut up and hop in. Let's take it for a spin."*

*He sounded lighthearted, but I saw the tension in his face. He wanted me to let the anger go and move on. I inhaled deeply and reached past the ache in my chest to focus on the car. A smile twisted my lips and I held out my hand. "Did Mike give you the keys?"*

The crinkle of paper brings me back to the present. I frown at the crumpled speakers receipt fisted in my palm. My sixteenth birthday card had shown up three days later, complete with a check for five grand. Three days had been just enough time for Samson to chew our parents out. Looks like this birthday hasn't turned out a total bust after all. I carefully smooth the receipt flat again, then slide it into my wallet, murmuring, "Thanks, big brother."

25

# CHAPTER 3

*The* hulking creature with a smashed snout and broad shoulders covered in aged armor-like red scales takes up the entire room's doorway.

Vile smoke puffs from his nose as his angry yellow eyes rake over the smaller green creature standing in the middle of the room.

He snorts his disapproval and his hooved feet stomp into the room to grab the young creature with soft, shiny green scales by the arm and yank him toward a partially made bed.

Roaring in fury, he rips off the covers and flings them to the floor, then yanks at the top sheet. His long claws dig into the bottom sheet, shredding it right off the bed.

As the green creature starts to wail, outrage turns the bigger one's yellow eyes red. He backhands the smaller one along his smashed maw before gesturing to the mess of covers and torn sheets on the floor.

Just when the younger one looks like he's about to speak, the red creature opens his mouth wide and spits a stream of molten fire all over the green one. The younger one's scales are too new. They don't protect him like an older creature's would.

*I yell and throw myself on the red attacker's back, fighting to turn his stream of fire away from the smaller one.*

*He reaches for me and his sharp claws dwarf my head as he digs them deep into my scalp and neck. I roar through the pain but tighten my hold on his thick neck, hoping to at least knock him out.*

*Instead he grabs hold of my head and excruciating pain scatters along my spine as he throws me forward like I weigh nothing.*

*I slam against the wall across the room and could've sworn I felt every bone in my back crack. Somehow I manage to land on my feet.*

*Groggy, I raise my fists and turn to face the red creature who's barreling toward me like a bull in an arena.*

The moment he hits, I yank fully awake, my heart and head pounding. I look at the clock, hoping it's time to get up. Four a.m. stares back at me. I force my eyes closed and try to will the headache away.

BLUE RIDGE's main office bustles with activity as I slip into a chair next to the door, crushing my schedule in a tight grip. Being surrounded by so many people in close quarters always makes me tense. I barely register the blur of students needing late slips or parent volunteers signing in for the morning. My head is still hurting from my nightmares, and now my ears are ringing as I quickly brush pebble dust from the cemetery's main entrance off the side of my shoe. It's not like I didn't expect the nightmares. It's just that I'd thought I was learning to handle them better. So much for that theory. I couldn't go back to sleep, so I left the house early and stopped by the cemetery to check Marcus' mother's headstone for a toy car. I made a promise and plan to keep it for as long as necessary.

Ten minutes later, as soon as the last person files out, the secretary starts to turn to me when a blonde girl strolls through the door, breezing past my chair.

"Hi," she says, flicking her gaze at me briefly before addressing the secretary. "Morning, Ms. Cresh."

"Good morning, Nara." The older woman chuckles. "What does Mr. Hallstead need this time? That man can never keep up with his paperwork."

I blink rapidly. Instead of blurring like everyone else does, in the brief second the girl looked at me, her features barreled through my headache, standing out in vivid clarity: bright green eyes, high cheekbones, and a wide smile. When the buzzing in my ears fades, I instantly straighten to watch her.

"You know him so well. Mr. Hallstead sent me to get more copies of the permission slips for the class field trip to Jamestown next week. He's run out and a few students still need to turn theirs in."

*Mr. Hallstead?* Sounds familiar. I skim the schedule in my hand. He's the teacher of the History class I'm here to switch out of so I can take the art class that's only offered in the fall.

Ms. Cresh hands her a stack of papers and once the girl leaves, the secretary smiles my way. "Okay, Mr. Harris. Now that the morning chaos is over, bring me your schedule and let's make that switch to the class you wanted."

Standing, I fold my schedule and tuck it into my back pocket. "Thanks, Ms. Cresh, but I think I'll just leave it as is. I'll take the art class next year."

Her brow furrows. "Are you sure? It's not a problem to switch it for you. We want your experience here to be a positive one."

Sympathy hangs in her tone, but I shake my head and let my gaze follow the blonde passing by the picture window as she walks down the hall. She's on the slender side and taller than the average girl, probably around five seven or eight. My lips quirk at her indoor soccer shoes peeking out from the bottom of her jeans. *An athlete, huh?* "I've always wanted to go to Jamestown," I murmur.

"Okay, then, Ethan. Let me give you a late note so you can get to class."

I take the note and head down the hall toward History, intrigued. For the first time in a very long time my thoughts are so occupied the buzzing in my head completely disappears.

I MAKE it through the rest of the day but not without growing more on edge with each passing hour. I have no idea when the images or voices will return, but the expectation alone is winding me up. When the final bell rings, I can't get out of school fast enough. Having the whole week off has spoiled me. It's been nice not to have to deal with school drama or people who can't keep their crap to themselves. Or digging into mine. I should've known I couldn't come to a new school without my past from Central following me.

Other than the secretary this morning, I haven't spoken to anyone all day. In each class, I found a seat in the back and stayed buried in my sketchpad to avoid eye contact. It's always easier if I keep to myself. Yet somehow rumors have already started to circle about why I'm starting at Blue Ridge after the school year has started.

At the end of the day, while pulling books from my locker, I overhear the full spectrum in low whispers not meant for my ears, yet they always seem to reach me.

"I heard he got kicked out of his last school."

"What school?"

"Central, I think."

"Bet he's into drugs."

"You know it's probably something juicy. I'm going to text my friend Rachel at Central and find out what she knows."

"Nah, he's just some prick who couldn't handle the heat."

I head out to my car and slip my earbuds in, cranking the tunes to blow out the annoyance. The last thing I need is to get into a fight on my first day of school. I have to find a way to keep myself together, on all fronts. I need to do this for Samson. From now on, the earbuds go in the second the last bell rings.

I stop short a few feet from my car, dumbfounded at the group of ravens hanging out on it like a tree branch. A burst of familiarity flickers in my chest. Have they followed me from the graveyard? This school's back parking lot is surrounded by trees, whereas my last school's parking lot wasn't, so maybe that's why, but still…it's odd and curious. Then my gaze zeroes in on the two spots of bird poop sitting on my roof and my temper rises, obliterating my curiosity. I wave my arm and bark at the birds, ignoring the sudden jolt of regret that flares when they startle and take flight.

JUST AS I'M about to turn into my neighborhood, I slam on the brakes. Three boys are bolting across the entrance, a snarling Rottweiler in fast pursuit.

I slowly turn into the neighborhood, my gaze following the kids and dog disappearing behind a house on the corner.

Pulling over to the side of the road, I park and get out. Deep, fierce growling echoes from the back of the house, punctuated by the boys' high-pitched squeals for someone to help.

I bolt after them and only stop for a second when my boot hits something in the middle of the road.

By the time I round the corner of the house, the muscular dog has the three boys, ranging in ages from eight to twelve, firmly trapped in a corner next to a gate. The kids must've thought they could get away from the dog inside the fence, but found the gate locked instead.

Hackles raised, back slightly arched, the dog stands about five feet back from the boys. Each time a kid makes a move, he hops in their direction and growls.

Finally the taller, chunky boy peers past his thick red bangs and sees me standing ten feet behind the dog. "Help! He's going to rip us to shreds."

His comment sets the younger two blond boys off in a bout of pitiful crying. They cling to each other, while the older one switches between keeping one eye on the dog and glancing at me with an imploring gaze.

I take a step forward and the growling dog startles at the sound of leaves crunching behind him. Wild, angry brown eyes shift my way, teeth bared. Something about his stance seems more vengeful than outright vicious. That's when I notice the right half of his snout doesn't lift as high as the left when he snarls. I can barely see his teeth on that side, but the teeth I do see are smeared with fresh blood.

He spreads his front legs and gives me a warning growl to stay back. "Easy, boy." I hold my hand up and take another step toward him.

Pain reflects in his eyes, and I feel his anger, especially toward the redhead, when he quickly flits his attention at the boy to make sure he hasn't moved.

As I move another step closer, the dog's steady gaze emits confusion and his bristling stance relaxes ever so slightly, enough that I can tell he's picking up on my calm tone, reacting to it. "I won't hurt you," I continue, lowering my hand to my side so he gets the message I'm no threat to him.

"You won't hurt *him*?" An incredulous voice squeaks near the gate. "He's attacking us!"

I frown at the older boy. "And whose fault would that be?"

He flushes and crosses his arms, braver now that I'm distracting the dog. "Wh—what are you talking about?"

I pull the slingshot I found on the road from my back pocket. "Is this yours?"

The kid juts his chin out, eyes defiant. "Yeah."

I rub my thumb along the top of the slingshot's handle. "I'm pretty sure you used this on the dog and that's why he chased you."

"Did not!" The kid glares at me with belligerent eyes, then jabs his finger toward the dog. "He just attacked us because he saw us running. Rotts are vicious. Everyone knows that."

As if in denial, the dog lets out a deep growl and takes a step in the kid's direction. The redheaded boy shrinks back toward the gate, yelling in a high-pitched voice, "Call him off!"

I tilt my head and hold the boy's gaze. "I will when you admit you attacked him."

"I didn't—" he starts to say, shaking his head in vigorous jerks.

"Yes, you did, David," the shortest blond boy pipes in, blue eyes glistening with a new round of terrified tears.

"Shut up, squirt—" the redhead says through clenched teeth.

The Rottweiler barks, then starts up a new long, low growl. The dog definitely sounds threatening, but I picked up the underlying tone and tried my best not to smile. He fully understands what's going on and is trying to intimidate the kid.

"Tell the truth so he'll make the dog go away," the other kid cuts in, eyeing the dog's new sounds warily. "And don't call my brother 'squirt.' Only I can call him that."

David sets his mouth in a tight line, then shrugs. "Fine. I hit the dog with a rock. Happy?"

I give him a cold smile. "Not yet. Apologize for hurting him."

David's brace-covered teeth separate in a wide gape. "I'm not apologizing to a stupid dog."

I take a few steps forward until I'm standing next to the dog. He's stopped growling. When he looks up at me, my gaze shifts to the brothers. "It's okay. You two can move over next to me."

With careful glances toward the dog, the younger boys sidle along the fence. Once they reach my side, I gently set my hand on top of the dog's big head and smile at him as he sits down on his haunches. I return my gaze to the other boy. "He's waiting, David."

David's gaze flits from the calmed dog to me. He shoves his hands into his jeans pockets, snark creeping into his expression. "He's fine. No harm, no foul."

I set my jaw and try not to lose my temper. "His lip is swollen and most likely his mouth is cut somewhere inside. You need to own up to your actions."

He glares and throws his hands wide. "I apologize...to the dog."

As I nod and grip the dog's collar, the kid steps away from the fence, braver now that I've got a hold of the dog. "You can give me my slingshot back."

"Sure," I say casually, and set the slingshot in his open hand. As soon as I let go of the bottom, the slingshot splits right down the middle of the handle, falling apart.

"Uh, you broke it! I'm going to tell my parents."

"Go right ahead." I adopt a brief smile. "I'll be happy to let them know how your slingshot ended up getting accidentally stepped on."

David glares at me and tosses the slingshot into the leaf-covered grass. Jerking his gaze to the boys next to me, he snarls, "Come on. Let's get out of here."

The two brothers fall in line with his footsteps, but I say quietly to the older one who's trailing behind, "You might want to pick a better friend. If I hadn't come along, this could've turned out very bad for you or your little brother."

Once the boys clear out, I lift my hand from the dog's head. He stares at me with a thankful gaze. I have no idea how I connect with animals. I've just always been able to. But unlike my newfound skill with the guitar, this talent I've never questioned. It's as easy and natural as breathing for me. I "sense" their needs. The dog's swollen lip makes me grind my teeth. While I rub his ears, I inspect his collar. No ID badge, but he at least *has* a collar. Someone owns and cares for him.

Walking away, I call over my shoulder, "Come on. There's an animal shelter near the strip mall. I'll bet they can give you stitches if you need them." When he doesn't follow right away, I look back. "I'm going to help you find your owner." Guess that's what he needed to hear, because he woofs and trots after me as if I've just promised him a juicy steak bone.

A WOMAN with curly blonde hair pulled back into a ponytail greets me with a smile as I escort the Rottweiler into the front lobby of the Central Virginia Animal Shelter (aka CVAS).

"Hello, there." She leans over the desk and eyes the Rottweiler sitting beside my feet. "Who do we have here?"

"I'm not sure." I point to his swollen lip. "A kid with a slingshot got him good. I was hoping someone could clean his wound and give him stitches if he needs them."

Her blonde eyebrows shoot up. "He's not your dog?"

I shake my head. "He doesn't have a tag, but he's wearing a collar. Do you have a chip reader? I'm hoping he has one so his owner can be contacted."

The woman grabs a handheld device, then waves for me to follow. I shadow her steps into a hall with two doors on each side. "I'm Sally. What's your name?" she says over her shoulder before she turns into the first room on the left.

"Ethan." I usher the dog into the exam room and he begins to pant once I shut the door behind us. I put my hand on his head and hold his wide-eyed, nervous gaze. "It's fine, boy."

When he sits and then leans against my thigh, Sally laughs and turns on the device she's holding. "He might not be yours, but he sure listens to you well."

I shrug. "He knows I won't let anyone hurt him."

Sally smiles as she runs the scanner along his back, looking for a chip. "Most animals get nervous when they come here because the smells remind them of going to the vet."

Cracking a smile, I scrub behind the dog's ear. "Well, there is that—"

The device beeps and Sally peers at the screen, then grins. "Ethan, we've got a number. Let me go check the registry."

Once she walks out, I sit down on the bench pushed against the wall. The dog ambles up and lays his chin on my knee. I chuckle. "Oh, is that how it's going to be? How are you supposed to look like a fierce dog if you keep giving me puppy eyes, hmmm?"

His only response is to tilt his head and lift his ears. I gently brush my fingers along his snout, inspecting the swelled skin. He whimpers but doesn't pull away.

"You going to let me look?" I ask right before I gently lift his lip. The skin inside resembles ground up hamburger. The rock must have jammed his upper lip against his teeth.

The dog turns his head sideways, laying his jaw across my knee to give me better access. I'm glad the bleeding seems to have stopped. Carefully lowering his lip back into place, I pat his neck before digging my fingers into his fur to give him a good scratch. "I'm sorry this happened to you, big guy. I get what it's like to be judged. Not any fun, is it?"

"You really have a way with animals," Sally says from the doorway.

I adopt a wry smile. "I understand them better than people."

"Rascal's owner is relieved we found him. He only lives ten minutes from here and is on his way. He asked me not to tend to his wounds, since he plans to take Rascal straight to his vet. As for understanding animals better." Sally bobs her head up and down as she walks into the room. "I totally get that. People are complex. Animals are—"

"Basic," I interject before she can say "simple." Animals are far from simple. I just get them on a fundamental level. People have way too much baggage to deal with.

She grins. "Yes, they're basic. Well put. It's amazing how one word—the *right* word—can say so much about them." Interest flickers in her eyes as her gaze flits over me. "Would you be interested in a volunteer position here, Ethan?"

Excitement stirs in my chest and I raise my eyebrows.

37

"Working with the animals, right? I'm not so good with people."

"Usually everyone has to work with the customers, but for someone with your natural ability, we'll make an exception." Sally does a little hop toward the door, then quickly looks back, eyes alight. "Don't go anywhere. I'm going to get the application."

*This* I can't screw up like everything else in my life. Volunteering here is exactly what I need to distract me from myself. I spread my hands wide and nod. "I'll be right here."

I'M LOOKING FORWARD to History class. The other day, the class had been halfway through by time I got there. I slipped in during the movie being played and found my way in the dark to a seat in the back. Thankfully the teacher didn't bother to introduce me. Makes it easier to just blend in as if I've always been there.

Today, I take my spot at the back of the room and watch the door, waiting for the girl from the office to walk in. Ms. Cresh had called her Nara. I dreamed about her last night, which is odd because I never dream about people I've *almost* met. Then again, she left a lasting impression that had stayed with me for two days straight.

The great thing about sitting in the back of the room is that you get to know a lot about your classmates without having to say a word to them. Facial expressions and body language tell many tales.

In the last forty minutes of History class on my first day, I learned that the two guys sitting in the left corner are a couple, the three football players in the farthest row on the right are dealing drugs, the two soccer players directly in front of me think of girls as walking blow-up dolls, and the flighty cheerleader in row two, seat number five, is smart, like brilliant smart, but she doesn't want anyone to know, especially the other cheerleaders.

Despite learning all that, I hadn't been able to glean much about the girl from the office. She faced forward the whole time and listened intently to the teacher's lecture.

I don't have to wait long for Nara to arrive this morning. The moment she walks in, I let out a long exhale and set my pencil down. I blink, surprised that her presence has such an arresting effect, but it does. For some reason I don't feel the desperate need to draw the images from my dreams so urgently.

Maybe it's because all the whispers flickering around in my head dissipate, or because taking in everything about her is pleasantly distracting. She's wearing faded jeans, a pink hoodie, and black boots. Today her hair is down, flowing past her shoulders. I want so badly to brush the straight blonde curtain aside so I can see her face better that I curl my fingers inward in my impatience.

When she pulls a purple pen out of her backpack, then glances around to make sure no one's near before she begins writing something on her palm, my lips twitch. I like her retro ways. Most girls take notes on their cell phones, but not this one. By the deep furrow in her brow, whatever she's jotting down is more important than some guy's phone number. It can't possibly be a homework assignment. She's only been to Homeroom so far. Whatever it is, she's got more than one thing on her mind. She writes several notes. I'm fully intrigued.

People start to file into the classroom. She looks up and I glance down, so she doesn't catch me staring. My gaze freezes on the paper. I've drawn a light outline of her profile in the corner of my page. I stare at the pencil in my hand as if it has a mind of its own. I don't remember picking it up.

The two soccer guys slide into their seats and the one with a buzz cut grabs my attention when he points to Nara and whispers to his friend, "I'm getting some of that."

The guy with shaggy blond hair snorts. "Good luck competing with a quarterback who could break you in half, Nate."

Nate's dark brows pull together. "She's with Jared?"

Who's Jared? I wonder as the blond guy shrugs and says, "I think she'd like to be. I've seen Nara and her friend Lainey sometimes hanging out and watching them practice."

"You want to do the redhead, Jake?" Nate asks, making a crude gesture.

Jake shrugs. "Sure, I've noticed Lainey. Bet she'd be fire in the sack, but I can't get her to give me the time of day. She's all about the football players."

"It's the quiet ones that surprise you." Nate nods toward Nara. "I'm so going to tap that, and I've got a plan to make it happen."

The pencil in my hand snaps in half as I listen to these two douches. I glance away, but ache to punch the Nate guy in the mouth just to shut him up. My fisted hands are shaking so bad I have to lock my fingers under the edge of my chair to stay seated.

"So what's your plan?" Jake asks, drawing my gaze back to them.

Nate leans close to his buddy and whispers, "I'm going to be her hero."

Jake chuckles. "And how are you going to make that happen?"

Nate takes on a smug look as he sits back in his seat. "An opportunity was laid out for me this morning. As I walked in late, I saw her back tire is almost flat. Must've caught a nail or something. By the time school's over, it'll be completely flat. Anyway, near the end of practice, I'm going to tell Coach I have a thing and need to leave early. I'll be there changing her tire for her when she's done with practice."

"You ah, need a jack and her spare to execute your grand plan. How're you going to get to them?"

"Easy. I've never seen her lock her car." Nate grins and holds his hand up in a high five. "She'll be mine before next weekend."

As the two asshats smack palms, my own itch to grab their necks and slam their skulls together. My gaze snaps to Nara, who's completely oblivious of the scheming going on about her. I set my jaw. There's no way I'll let that jerk-off anywhere near her.

# CHAPTER 4

*I*n the afternoon, I pull my car into a parking space far enough away from Nara's car not to be noticed, but close enough to keep hers in my line of sight. Resting my wrist across the steering wheel, I watch as Nate shows up still in his soccer gear. When he walks around the back of Nara's car and sees her back tire fully inflated, he lets out a string of curses and kicks the tire with his cleat. I savor the moment as he glares around the parking lot, looking for the culprit who ruined his "look like a hero" plan.

After he stalks off to his car, I start the engine and pull out of the parking lot, heading to Mike's Body Shop with Nara's flat tire in my trunk. I'll have the tire repaired and switched back out with her full spare before her soccer practice is done tomorrow afternoon. I might not be able to be a part of Nara's life like a normal guy, but even something as small as keeping an eye out for her feels good.

Over the next couple of days, I catch glimpses of Nara interacting with her friends in study hall and outside of class in the locker hall. When I overhear her mooning over that

Jared guy with her friend Lainey, I inwardly roll my eyes. I've seen Jared with his football buddies. He's only marginally a step up from the two jerks who sit in front of me in History.

A part of me can't help but wonder what it would be like to get to know Nara better, to be a friend she likes to hang with. I know *my* life would be better for knowing her. Nara shines. That's the only word that comes to mind when I think of her. It's not that she's the perkiest person in the world, but she tries to see the best in people. I'd have written that redhead Lainey off a long time ago, but Nara sees something in her seemingly one-dimensional friend. She reaches deep for the good in others, which is an effort I gave up on.

Nara's positive outlook draws me in, but it also makes me feel the need to protect her from herself. She'd have taken Nate's sincerity about fixing her tire at face value without a thought that he had an underlying motive for his actions. It's as if she's never had anything bad happen to her, never had a need to build a protective wall. I've learned the hard way that sometimes defenses are necessary, more for the unknown dangers than the expected ones.

The way I've begun to feel about Nara scares me. After only a few days, I sense the moment she enters the room. I don't even have to look up. It doesn't matter that a roomful of people separate us, I'm suddenly more alert and my heart starts racing. She still calms me, but in a peaceful, clearing my head kind of way. Concentrating on my drawings becomes impossible when I know she's present.

I'm fiercely attracted to Nara, but the difference between Nate and me is, I'd give anything to get to know the *real* her. The person she doesn't project to the world. I have a feeling she runs much deeper. Those notes she writes on her hand tell me so.

Every time I convince myself to try to meet Nara's gaze

in the hall, I remember my issues and stare straight ahead. It's been easier to forget them while I'm at school, since things seem to be a bit more manageable lately. I've only had a few spaced-out episodes. I hate that I can't control what's going on with me. How can I hope to start a friendship with Nara and get to know more about her when nothing about myself is worth talking about? What's the point of opening the door? It's better to have never known what it's like to have Nara look happy to see me than to have that look disappear from her eyes. Wishes by their nature might remain unfulfilled, but they can also never be taken away.

I WALK in from school to the sound of the phone ringing. I rush to answer, mainly because I'm surprised to hear it. Our phone rarely rings. Over the past six months, my brother has taken to keeping telemarketers on the phone as long as possible. He'll string them along for a good twenty minutes, then tell them he's not interested and promptly hang up. Telemarketers must have their own "do not call" list reserved for special cases like my mocking brother.

"Hello?" I say quickly.

"Ethan?"

Everything inside me freezes. I haven't heard my dad's voice in a long time.

"You there, son?"

I squeeze my eyes shut and ignore my pounding heart as I take slow, quiet breaths. "Yes."

My dad clears his throat. "Well, I'm calling because I see the check we sent you hasn't cleared the bank yet. That's a lot of money to just be floating around, Ethan."

My pounding heart stutters, and resentful fire streaks

along the inside of my chest. "Sorry to mess up your finances."

"My finances—"

"Just consider the check void."

"What!" My dad's voice rises. "Now you listen to me, young man—"

"That's the great thing about not living with you." I squeeze the phone tight and the handset creaks against my palm. "I don't have to listen."

"Godamnit, Ethan—"

I slam the phone down so hard the handset breaks apart in pieces. The phone starts to ring again, but this time the ringer sounds sick, like it's dying. The first phone call in two years and he doesn't even ask how I've been? In one fell swoop, my dad has thoroughly snuffed out any hope that my parents still care. I clench my jaw and unplug the base from the wall while it's still ringing. I was wrong. Wishes can be taken away if you're stupid enough to open the damned door.

I wonder what my parents told the neighbors about my sudden disappearance. Probably that I was studying abroad for the rest of my high school career, trying to make me sound all worldly and cosmopolitan. God forbid the truth would come out.

The idea of staying home right now makes me twitchy, like I'm going to crawl out of my own skin. I don't want to face Samson. Don't want to explain the smashed phone. Don't want to deal. At all. I quickly jot down a note to my brother, telling him I'll be out late at the library.

When I pull out of the driveway, I crank up my new speakers as loud as I can take it. A few miles down the road, the music still isn't enough to drown out the angry, resentful thoughts ricocheting inside my head.

Even though I vowed never to go back to McCormicks, that's exactly where I end up. And this time, Chance is late for practice—some kind of fender bender—so I hop onstage among the other band members and drown out my frustrations with a borrowed guitar.

The guys are amazed by my ability to add flair to their rock music with my own unique style. My fingers go numb with the speed I'm picking out the notes, but this time I don't question it. I just close my eyes and let the music flow out.

By the time I come back to reality, Chance is there, playing the keyboards, adding even more depth to the Southern rock song we're playing. Sweat trickles under my hair along my temples, and I realize it's due to the hot stage lights that currently blare down on us. *When did they turn them on?* My arms feel like jelly as Duke and I end the song with hard, reverberating sounds.

The sudden roar of the crowd startles me and I blink against the bright lights. *Holy shit! I'm performing?* I thought we were still practicing. I stand and hit the mic someone has placed in front of me as I turn to hand the guitar to Ivan.

I'm ready to bolt, but he jerks his head back and forth in hard shakes. "No way you're leaving now, man. They're eating this shit up." Pointing one of his sticks at me, he says, "And no more holding back on us. That deep voice of yours has them squirming."

*Deep voice?* I glance at the mic, then to Dom, who's grinning. "Keep up those backup vocals, Adder."

As Ivan begins to tap his drumsticks together to count out the tempo of the next song, my gaze snaps to Chance, who nods toward the guitar in my hand with serious eyes. "Get to it. We're rockin' a new sound tonight and we've got a crowd to please."

I try not to think about the people watching beyond the

spotlights as I drag a shaky hand through my damp hair and sit down with the guitar once more. Even though my voice is decent, I *never* sing. It's too open, too personal. I start to strum the guitar and as the strings' vibrations resonate, a surge of nostalgic familiarity—a sense of rightness—rises up inside me, but this time I vow to stay cognizant through the experience. At least, I hope I can.

When we finish the set and the crowd's individual voices break through my consciousness, calling for "more", I work hard not to let the others see me shaking all over. Remaining perfectly still is exhausting, but somehow I manage because, at least for now, I haven't thought about my parents at all.

Once we run through another set and Dom tells the crowd we're taking a half-hour break, this time I hand the guitar to Ivan, saying, "I've got to go. I have school tomorrow."

He grunts, then nods and takes the guitar. I've just stepped off the stage when Dom hops down beside me. Pulling me to the side, he says, "Any time you want to perform with us, you're welcome," as he shoves something in my hand.

I frown at the two twenties and try to hand them back to him. "What's this for?"

Dom curls my fist around the money. "Hell no, kid. You earned your keep tonight. Though next time…have a beer. It'll help you loosen up sooner."

I stiffen. "I don't drink." *I'm messed up enough.*

Dom shrugs. "Suit yourself." Glancing toward the group of girls who've moved over to talk to the band, he snorts. "Seriously though, I know you can't always practice with us because of classes and stuff, but your talent is phenomenal. Even Duke, who's usually a total ass about accepting outsiders, can't discount your skill. Tonight was off the charts."

*But it's not* my *talent.* I want to yell at the top of my lungs. Instead I calmly say, "Thanks for letting me crash, Dom. I really needed this tonight."

He claps me on the shoulder and winks. "We all win. Keep the money, Adder. And we hope we'll see you again next week. You can help turn the *e* in Weylaid to an *a*."

Laughing at his cleverness, Dom hops back onstage to address the fans crowding around. I turn to leave, but two college-age girls—a redhead and a brunette—are standing in front of me.

"Ohmygod, you were amazing! We heard them call you Adder. Is that your real name? So cool. We've never seen you here before. Did you just join the band?" the redhead babbles.

"I just fill in sometimes," I say in a low tone. I'm starting to feel edgy and really want to leave, but these girls are blocking my way.

"When will you be here again?" The brunette, who's wearing a t-shirt that reads ***Weylaid and hooked!*** tucks a strand of hair behind her ear and slides a sideways glance to her friend.

I shrug. "Not sure."

"Well, here's my name and number," the redhead says. Before I can say anything, she grabs my hand and quickly scrawls the name Sheryl and a number on my palm. "Call me the next time you'll be performing. I'll come just to hear that sexy voice."

For a brief second I picture the girl standing in my personal space, writing her name and number on my hand, with blonde, shoulder-length hair, brilliant green eyes and a wide smile. What I wouldn't give to have Nara look at me this way.

Pulling my hand from hers, I say, "I'm glad you enjoyed the show. If you'll excuse me, I've got to go."

Would Nara be attracted to the music like these girls are? I can't help but wonder as I walk out of McCormicks into the cool night air and stroll down the brickyard mall.

But it's not real, I mentally argue with myself. *It's not me. I'm not even using my real name. I would never tell Nara about this. I want her to get to know the* real *me.* Yes, my fingertips are still tingling, proving I'm the one who played the instrument, but I can't get past feeling like an imposter. It's sad that a talent I didn't personally develop is somehow helping me cope. It doesn't make any sense, yet I can't deny how good it feels to escape from myself for a few hours.

At this pub, I'm an unknown. No one I know comes here, because they're either not old enough to drink or they're older than the college crowd. Since my old friends have been banned—knowing them, probably indefinitely—it's the perfect place to get lost.

On my way to the parking garage, I cut through the alley I usually do as I focus on the benefits of continuing to play with this band every so often. Not only can I make some additional cash, but if this helps me feel somewhat normal, maybe I can carry that off at school. My nights might've gotten worse lately, but at least things have been better during the day. I really want to get to know Nara—

Two guys jump me at once, throwing me against a brick wall. As I try to regain my equilibrium, one of them grabs me and pulls my arms back, while the other slams a fist into my face. My head snaps sideways and pain explodes across my jaw as the stocky guy with a ham fist snarls to his buddy. "Take his wallet."

"Don't touch me." I wrench the words out and twist my hip to make it hard for the guy to get to my wallet tucked in my front pocket. I can't see either of their faces. It's just too dark.

I hear what sounds like a switchblade flipping open and the bigger guy rumble, "Have it your way, prick. We'll leave you bleeding out then."

I turn my head and listen past the guy holding me for the bigger guy's movements. When he shuffles forward quickly, I sense the blade arcing toward me. On instinct I swing my foot wide, kicking hard. The sound of metal clattering to the street reverberates in the alley and my attacker yells, "Fuck you!"

As the stocky guy swings a fist toward my head again, the air seems to bend and shift, telling me his movements. I duck just in time and he hits his friend in the shoulder instead. The force knocks him back, ripping his grip from my arms.

"Sonofabitch, Ray! You hit *me.*" the skinnier guy yells as he pushes himself off the brick wall he's fallen against.

I'm suddenly free, but I see the bigger guy's outline coming toward me, fast and furious. Instead of running, I act on instinct and kick him in the gut.

"Stay back," I grit out as he stumbles several steps, then rights his feet underneath him.

He howls and launches his hefty bulk in my direction at the same time the skinny one lands on my back. Even though I stagger under his weight tugging on my shoulders, a surge of pure adrenaline and self-preservation kicks in. I broaden my stance and plow my fist into the bigger guy's oncoming face.

He flies across the wide alley, slamming into the opposite brick wall. As he slowly falls to the ground unconscious, his buddy wails in my ear. "Shit! You okay, Ray?"

The skinny guy hammers his fist on my shoulder, then snakes his thin arm around my neck in a chokehold. I snarl and tug hard at the same time I twist him away from me, intending to fling him off.

Something snaps right before his body sails down the alley to land hard in a rolling heap. I gape at the distance he lands; there's a good thirty feet between us. My mind screams at the impossible distance I've thrown him, while my heart jumps in my throat at the reality I can't blink away. The defensive strength and ferocity of my fighting shocks me. My breath saws in and out while I clench and unclench my shaking hands, trying to calm myself enough to listen.

*Please, please. I didn't accidently kill him, did I?* When I hear a low moan come from his direction, and then a pitiful whine saying, "I think my arm's broken," I exhale a relieved breath and bolt from the alley.

I break every speed limit on my way home. As soon as I reach my street, I force my foot to lighten on the gas pedal and finally pull into the driveway like I'd just come from the library. Shutting off my engine, I jam the heels of my palms against my eyes and try to calm my racing heart. Just when I think I might be able to act somewhat normal, this craziness happens.

*You're fine. Breathe. Breathe. Mothers have lifted cars off their babies before. Sheer self-preservation and adrenaline amped you up, that's all.* But no amount of rationalization can erase the fact that violence had erupted from me on instinct, like it had a mind of its own.

In my dreams, I accept the darkness that wells up in me, because my dreams are screwed up beyond measure. To experience that loss of control in the real world scares me more than anything. I really need to avoid fighting from now on. Otherwise, I might actually kill someone.

I take several more breaths and realize that the lights are on in the living room. My brother's waiting up. Tonight I'll probably have the mother lode of horrific dreams, so as much as I'd like to use the excuse that I'm tired, the last thing I want to do is go to bed anytime soon. With a sigh of grudging acceptance, I pull the keys from the ignition and open my car door. Suddenly, dysfunctional family drama doesn't seem so hard to face anymore.

# CHAPTER 5

*I* walk into the house and my gaze instantly seeks my brother sitting on the couch. Beer bottle in hand, he's flipping through the channels. The moment the door closes behind me, he clicks off the TV and slowly swivels my way. "Hey."

It's just one word, but it conveys a lot. He's still in his work clothes and drinking a beer at quarter 'til eleven. He rarely drinks, let alone this late. I sigh inwardly and stroll over to the living room, hands tucked in my jeans pockets.

"Want to talk about that?" Samson nods his blond head toward the broken phone bits now displayed on the coffee table like some kind of abstract art.

"Not particularly." I pull two twenties out of my pocket and set them on the table. "That should cover replacing it."

Samson frowns. He wants to ask where I got the money, but sighs instead.

"Don't worry. I got it legally."

His blond eyebrows shoot up. "I didn't ask—"

"You didn't have to." I shrug and look away from his probing gaze. "I have a couple of jobs going right now."

Samson smiles, his shoulders relaxing into the couch as he leans back to cross an ankle over his knee. "That's great. Just remember to fill out the tax forms, okay?"

Shoving my hands back in my pockets, I rock on my heels. "One job's volunteer and the other's not official. Just cash when I chip in here and there."

"Ah." Samson nods, setting the beer bottle on his bent knee.

When a heavy silence descends between us, I start to turn, saying, "It's late. I've got school tomorrow—"

"Eth..."

I turn back to him.

"What happened to your face?" Samson suddenly sits up on the couch.

I forgot to keep that side of my face hidden from him. I flash a confident smile. "You should see the other guy."

"You promised no more fights."

I hate the disappointed look on his face, so I wave as if it's no big deal. "Was just goofing off with guys from my old school. I'm fine. What were you going to say?"

He eyes me doubtfully for a second, then nods. "Dad called me." When I don't speak, he continues, "I don't blame you for being mad—"

I throw my hands out, my stance stiff. "Then why are we having this conversation?"

"Because it's the first time he's called since you came to live with me."

"And do you know what he said?" I grate. "He wanted to know why I hadn't deposited his check."

Samson blinks before saying in a quiet tone, "If you ever

want to mend fences, sometimes you have to reach across to the other side."

"Why should I make the effort? He hasn't." I fist my hands by my side. "Not once in two fucking years."

Samson sets his mouth in a grim line. "I know exactly how much of an ass he can be, Ethan. I lived with him too. It's because I know him that I'm asking you to consider making the first move. Prove that you're not just as stubborn as him."

"You barely speak to them yourself," I shout.

Samson doesn't react to my outburst, other than a stiffening of his shoulders. Ever since I can remember, his relationship with our father has always been contentious, which eventually affected his relationship with our mom too.

A memory of Samson storming out the front door during one of his rebellious teenage arguments with my dad flashes through my mind. The moment the door slammed closed, my father swung his pinched, disapproving expression my way. "Your brother will probably end up in jail before he's twenty. Thank God one of you seems to have a level head on your shoulders." My stomach pitches as the memory reminds me that I eventually disappointed them far more than Samson ever had.

*Why is my brother defending him?* As I watch Samson's jaw muscle twitch, a sudden realization crashes over me, quickly followed by a heavy wave of guilt; my brother would never admit it, but *I'm* the reason their tenuous relationship is nonexistent.

How do you forgive someone for not believing in you? How do you get past the hurt and anger, especially when they refuse to take responsibility for their part? I stare at the muscle giving away Samson's unease. You consider the possibility for your brother.

"I'll think about it," I finally say. When Samson starts to nod, I say in a gruff voice as I turn toward the stairs, "I said 'think.' It's late. I'm going to bed."

After I lay in bed, I force my eyes wide open in the dark and stare at the spot of light on the ceiling coming from a lamp light outside. Anything to stay awake as long as possible. Eventually thoughts of what happened in the alley and issues with my dad start to creep into my emptied mind, so I distract myself by switching all my thoughts to Nara.

She'd find a way to forgive her father. She's just that kind of person, always trying to see the good in others. Why do I always focus on the bad stuff? I hate zeroing in like I do. I can't even see the good in my own father. The thought makes me frown and squirm against my bed. The movement sets off an itchy sensation along my shoulder blade. Must be from that scuffle in the alley. I did slam against that brick wall pretty hard. Probably irritated the skin there.

I scratch my shoulder and roll over, turning my thoughts back to Nara. She'd probably be a bit freaked out if she knew I sketch her in class sometimes. I can't help it. She's far more interesting to draw than the disturbing images from my dreams. The continued itching pulls my musings back to what happened in the alley. That whole experience depresses me the more I think about it. It proves I can't be a part of Nara's life now no matter how desperately I wish I could.

The knowledge sits on my chest like a hundred pound weight. As I sink deeper into my bed, my back starts burning. The sensation is so annoying, I stumble out of bed and into the hall bathroom in the dark. Grabbing the cortisone from the cabinet, I slap a layer of the cream on my shoulder, then fall back in my bed where I finally close my eyes.

Since Nara can't be a part of my real life, maybe if I fall

asleep thinking about her, she'll show up in my dreams like she did that one night after my first day of school.

WHY IS it when you convince yourself to stop thinking about someone, you instead hyper focus on her? It's like the darker I see myself, the more attractive Nara's lightness becomes. And now that my focus is razor sharp, I'm starting to notice little things I never had before.

We're in the middle of a history lecture, and I've spent most of the morning drawing. Unlike my strange new musical skills, sketching is a talent I developed over time. Embracing my comfort zone sometimes helps mute the noise in my head. Unfortunately, the gravelly voice has been incessant since I got to school.

*Eeeethan,* he whispers in my head, moving from one ear to the other in stereo surround sound. *Why are you drawing so vigorously? You really don't want to understand. I've told you the easiest thing to do. Why don't you listen—*

I glance up at Nara, thinking I might draw her to distract myself. The second I look at her, the voice cuts off. I blink at the surprising silence just as Nara moves her notebook and her elbow sends her pencil rolling to the edge of her desk. The pencil rolls off, but she never looks away from her notebook as she quickly reaches down and grabs the pencil mid-fall between two fingers.

When she starts flipping the pencil casually around her thumb over and over, like she didn't just perform something as odd as catching a fly with chopsticks, my eyebrows shoot up. How many people could've done that? Sure, some people could've caught a falling pencil in their palm without looking, but to snag a falling object between the tips of your fingers without looking took *some* kind of talent. I rub my jaw. Then again, it's possible she just got lucky.

After class, while standing in front of my locker pulling out books for the next set of classes, I hear Nate scheming with Jake again about his desire to hook up with Nara.

"I've got a new 'Nara' plan," Nate whispers to Jake after he flicks him on the back of the head.

Jake rubs his head as he shuts his locker. "Maybe you should give it up, bud. She's pretty into her adoration of Jared. Heard her talking to Lainey just yesterday about him."

"Jared's an ass. The arrogant prick thinks he can have any girl he wants."

I pull my chin toward my chest and curl my lips inward, mentally snarling my mutual agreement with Nate's assessment of Jared.

Jake snorts and jams his shoulder into Nate's. "He thinks that because it's true, asswipe."

The two guys scuffle for a couple seconds, then Nate says, "No, seriously, here's the plan. I'm going to hang out and watch her practice. Then when it's over, I'm going to praise her soccer skills and ask her for some pointers…you know, goalie to goalie. You can come too and say similar shit to Lainey. We might get a twofer out of this."

Jake snorts. "You *could* learn a thing or two from Nara. I've heard she's pretty much unstoppable in the goal."

"That's 'cause girls don't kick as hard as guys." Nate snickers and rubs his hands together. "But yeah, I think it's a great excuse. I'll stroke her ego and then later she'll stroke mine."

As he laughs at his own joke, a sudden urge to grab him and slam his head into my locker rushes through my mind. I clench my jaw and tamp down my anger when an ironic idea pushes past the violent thoughts, settling some of the coiled tension.

WATCHING Nara practice soccer isn't part of my "derail Nate's plan" idea. I know I'll get nostalgic since I really miss playing. But after Jake's comment to Nate about Nara's talent, my curiosity is piqued. At least, that's what I tell myself. My avid interest has nothing to do with needing another excuse to watch Nara in action.

Instead of executing my plan immediately after Nate heads off to soccer practice, I climb to the highest bleacher in the stadium and pretend to watch the football practice going on. The whole time, my line of sight stays locked on the soccer field adjacent to the stadium where the girls practice.

Appreciating Nara's athleticism completely absorbs me for the first half of the practice, but after following every move she makes, I'm mystified. She hasn't made a single error. Not one dive in the wrong direction. When it comes to one-on-one, no one seems to be able to juke her out or get past her. It's only when she's surrounded by most of the opposing team that she's beaten.

I sit up straighter and shrug off my Nara fascination to watch her practice with an unbiased eye. Again and again, she makes another last-minute dive to snag the ball before it goes in. This time, I study her moves with skepticism. No one is *that* good, no matter how much they practice. It's statistically impossible. Is she watching their eyes? Reading the players for visual cues?

Nara's in another one-on-one situation, and just when my suspicions are about to be confirmed once more, she makes a bonehead move, falling across the goal in the wrong direction. As the ball clears past her into the net, my gaze narrows. Nara had no reason to dive the way she did. I might not be able to see the offensive player's expression from here, but everything about her body language, from the position of her hips to her planted foot's stance, screamed that she'd kick the ball to the right. Yet Nara dove to the left side of the goal. Why?

*Because she dove that way on purpose.* I'm thoroughly surprised at the possibility that flickers through my mind. When Nara does the same thing a few minutes later, a slight smile lifts my lips and I murmur, "I *knew* you had layers." My attention slides to the male soccer player standing along the edge of the soccer field, watching the girls practice. *And you are so screwed,* I mentally address Nate as I make my way down the bleachers.

Once I let the air out of all four of Nate's tires—he's lucky that's all I did. It took all my willpower not to shred them—I place a printed note behind the wiper on his windshield.

*Good girls have guardian angels, known as Protection and Vengeance.*
*It would be best for you to move on. You don't want to meet*
*Vengeance.*

*Protection*

The girls' soccer practice is almost over, so I bump my hip against Nate's car to set off the alarm, then quietly whistle as I make my way to my car parked in a neighborhood across the street from the school.

I'm still whistling when I walk into CVAS a half hour later.

"There you are." Sally turns from the filing cabinet

behind the desk, manila folder in hand. "I'm so glad you're here on time. We've just got two more dogs in. Six dogs need baths this afternoon, so you'll be tag-teaming with William in the bathing area."

Even learning I'll be spending the next three hours up to my elbows in dog hair and shampoo suds doesn't dampen my mood. "That's fine, Sally."

She nods toward the back. "William is already back there. He'll point the ones out for you."

Once I pass through the door and enter the hall, William is standing in the main kennel room, his shirt wet from the dog he's just bathed. As I stroll toward him, he latches the clean dog inside. "One down, five more to go," he says with a grimace, glancing up at me.

I shrug. I'm used to doing this job myself. "Which other ones need to be bathed?"

Shoving his floppy blond hair back from his forehead, William retrieves a black lab mix from her kennel, then nods toward the cage next to that one. "I've moved all the dogs who need to be bathed into this row of cages for now. We'll move them back to their regular kennels once they're dry."

William heads back through the heavy swinging door that leads to the bathing area as I turn to the other dogs. Three of the four remaining dogs turn imploring brown eyes my way and begin to bark as if saying, "Pick me! Pick me! I want your attention, but does it have to be at the expense of enduring a bath?"

I glance past the beagle, chihuahua and chow/shepard mix to the black and brown mutt that looks like a boxer mated with a lab. He's lying down with his chin on his paws. I stroll past the excited dogs, wondering at his laidback attitude with all the barking and chaos going on around him.

The moment I step within a few feet of his cage, a wave

of sad acceptance overwhelms me. I stumble under the weight of it, but then continue forward with determined steps. I walk right up to the cage and open it, saying to the dog, "Come on, boy. Let's go outside."

He lifts his head and perks his ears at the mention of the word "outside," then sighs and slowly lowers his chin back to his white-tipped paws, brown eyes locked on me.

Without a word, I gather his seventy-pound bulk in my arms and carry him out the back door.

When the heavy door shuts behind us, cutting off the din inside the kennel area, the dog rapidly sniffs the scents in the brisk air, then settles his cheek against my arm and takes a deep breath.

"I know," I say as I carry him toward the big oak trees standing guard along the fence line at the back of CVAS's property.

He seems to grow heavier with each step I take, but I manage to sit down next to one of the trees with him still in my arms. As I lean my back against the tree, I lower his feet to the ground.

He looks lost and confused, like he doesn't understand why I'm not holding on to his scruff or why I haven't put a leash on him. "Tonight's your night." Reaching out I scratch behind his ear and ask, "How about I call you Buddy. What do you want to do?"

He stares longingly at the woods past the fence and I stop petting him to give him a choice. "You can go there if you want to, or you can stay with me."

When he just tucks his legs under him and lays his chin on my thigh, I blink back tears and swallow the knot until it rolls down my throat, tightening my chest. "Okay, Buddy." My voice is gruff with emotion as I lay my hand on the top of his head, then slide my palm along his neck and back. "We'll just hang for as long as you want."

A few minutes pass and the night sounds grow quiet. I don't even feel the cool air on my bare arms as I continue to stroke along his fur. He's enjoying my attention and closes his eyes, giving me his trust. In return I give him affection for as long as I can.

William bursts through the back door, glancing all around. When he finally spots us, he strides over, looking flustered. "I wondered where you went. Come on. Let's go."

"I can't help tonight, William."

"You have to help, Ethan," he huffs and flails his skinny arms. "I can't bathe three more dogs *alone*."

"Then get someone else." I pat Buddy's uplifted head back down to my thigh, then meet William's gaze with a pointed one. "I came out here where it's quiet for a reason."

"We'll just see about that." William screws up his face. "I'm not doing all the work tonight because you've decided to be lazy."

Once he stomps off and goes back inside, I chuckle when Buddy inches even closer so I can run my hand all the way down his back. "Like that, do you?"

A few minutes later Sally casually walks to the back of the property. The spotlight behind her head makes all the curly pieces of hair falling out of her ponytail look like a messy halo. She is kind of like an angel to these animals. The thought makes me smile a little.

"Hey, Ethan. I really need you to help William tonight."

I shake my head. "Any other night I would, but not tonight." I glance down at the dog I'm petting. "Tonight is his night."

Sally's knees creak as she kneels to pat the dog's head. "We have a responsibility to all the animals," she says gently.

"We can't just pick and choose which ones we give our love to."

I meet her sympathetic gaze with a steady one. "We do when it's their last night."

"Last night?" She glances down at the dog, then raises her eyebrows in happy surprise. "If you're going to adopt him, that's wonderful. You can give him all this extra love tomorrow, but tonight the other dogs are waiting—"

"He won't make it until tomorrow. He's dying."

"How do you know?" Sally tilts her head, looking doubtful. "I know you have an amazing instinct with them, but—"

"Please get someone else to help tonight. I won't be coming back in until he's gone. Buddy deserves to take his last breath surrounded by affection, not a cage."

Sally bites her lip and starts to nod when Hailey, a girl who answers the phone and takes care of administrative paperwork up front, pokes her head out the door. "Sally, Nara's here. She wants to talk to you about working her in around her soccer schedule."

Sally's face brightens as she pushes herself back to a standing position. "Tell her I'll be right there, Hailey."

My heart jerks. "Is that Nara Collins?" I ask, my voice taut with worry for the dog and elated surprise that Nara might work here.

"Yes, Nara Collins. Do you know her?"

I shrug and try to act casual. "No, but I've seen her around school."

Sally's shoulders relax and she smiles. "Nara will stay and help with the bathing if I ask her to, so she just saved you tonight, Ethan."

Seems to be an unintentional habit of hers, I think as I lower my gaze and say solemnly, "Thank you for giving Buddy and me some time."

Nodding to the dog, she says, "I hope you're wrong about him."

My hand pauses mid-rub along his tense rib cage. "I'm not."

The dog seems to relax once Sally closes the door behind her. I sit with him for over two hours. When his breathing starts to slow, yet his body continues to flex and spasm under my hand, I say, "It's okay to let go, Buddy."

His big brown eyes lock with mine and I feel his pain and the tension inside him as self-preservation continues to make him fight, even when his organs have already given up. Cancer or some other kind of disease has ravaged him from the inside. I'm glad I came to work today so I could give Buddy some relief during his last moments. "Take a deep breath." I pat him gently and speak past the ache in my chest. "Then just exhale slowly. I'm here all the way."

As Buddy struggles to take his last breath, I don't hold back the tears any more. I think about how much we have in common. Just like Buddy, I don't have anyone in my life who would shed tears of understanding and acceptance over me if I were dying. I know my brother cares for me because I'm family, but I want someone who understands me, the *real* me, and loves me despite my weirdness. "Maybe one day, Buddy," I whisper to his suddenly still body.

Sally is waiting for me in the back room when I carry Buddy inside. We're the only employees left at the shelter as I lay his limp body down on the blanket she's prepared for him. Tears make tracks down her round cheeks while she runs her hand along Buddy's fur. Glancing up at me, she says in a sincere tone, "I won't doubt you again, Ethan. It's rare when we lose one, but it never gets any easier. Thank you for giving him love when he needed it most."

# CHAPTER 6

$\mathscr{I}$'m supposed to be collecting books for the first half of the day, but instead I'm leaning on my open locker door in zombie mode from the lack of sleep the night before. When my unfocused gaze suddenly sharpens, I know; Nara's somewhere close.

My heart rate ramps up and I start scanning for her blonde head. Finally my eyes land on her on the opposite end of the hall as she turns into the locker area with Lainey. She's talking fast and waving her hands in full-on animation over whatever story she's relaying to her friend.

I watch them weave through the throng, my gaze tracking around people blocking my vision. It's when I move my head to keep Nara in my line of sight that I notice something that makes my heart jerk. As they make their way to the middle of the chaotic crowd, Lainey's been jostled at least five times, but no one has touched Nara.

While Nara rambled, she ducked under a guy spinning a basketball on his finger, twisted her shoulder to avoid being jammed by a swinging trombone case, and then at the very last second she leaned into Lainey as if to tell her something important at the exact moment a football player vaulted into the air and arched backward in order to snag a football one of his teammates had thrown across the crowd. If she hadn't moved to the side at that exact moment, he would've plowed her over like a bowling pin.

Nara didn't have a tense, anticipatory look on her face as she made her way down the hall; she moved intuitively. It was like watching a stuntman act out a fight scene in a movie, perfectly coordinated. *How has no one ever noticed this about her?*

When Nara and Lainey pass by, Nara glances my way and says, "Hi."

I want to say "hey" back, but the word jams in my throat. I'm just so stunned by my sudden realization. My gaze tracks the girls until they turn the corner, while incredulous wonder flits through me. Lainey seemed completely oblivious to Nara's synchronized movements. So even Nara's best friend doesn't know she's special?

I might've missed an opportunity to speak to Nara, but I feel as if I just downed an energy drink. I shut my locker, hiding a pleased smile.

WHAT I LEARNED this morning stays with me all day. It really starts to bug me in study hall, because I still don't know how Nara does what she does. When I saw her playing soccer yesterday, I couldn't see her expressions from a distance, but after watching her eyes this morning, I dismiss my first "she reads body language" impression. Now my theory is that she has some kind of intuitive ability. Which is all it is...just a theory. It's not like I can walk up and ask her, but there's another way to find out.

The last bell rings, signaling the end of the day. My feet take me down the hall toward the main atrium, but then I hear a shout and I look over. Nara and her teammates are goofing off with a soccer ball in the hall. Suddenly the perfect opportunity presents itself, and I find myself heading in their direction.

As one of the soccer players kicks the ball hard, Nara twists sideways and bolts after it. I blend into the small group of people walking through the hall. Nara doesn't notice me pick up my speed to move directly behind her. Since I'm out of her line of sight, I've eliminated her ability to read physical cues, which gives me the chance to put this "intuitive ability" theory to the test. I speed up a bit more, then veer directly into her path.

I didn't expect Nara to glance my way at the last second, but she does. Surprise flits across her features and she yells, "Look out!" I adjust slightly, and she zooms by so close I catch a whiff of sunshine and flowers.

But her appealing smell isn't what briefly slows my pace. It's the electric sensation that runs through me as our bodies nearly collide. Hot and cold shoots from my head to my feet in rapid succession, right before laser-sharp awareness zips up my spine and seizes my lungs.

Nothing I felt about her before, none of the tingling sensations I experienced whenever she entered the same room, compare to this powerful connection. The surreal moment leaves an indelible pulling impression behind, like she actually snagged a piece of my soul as she blew past. *Holy shit that was intense.* As elation and shock slam through me, it takes supreme effort not to meet her gaze with questions in my eyes.

All of this happens in milliseconds, leaving me shaking inside, but I force an impassive expression. Hooking the runaway ball with my foot, I send it her way, then keep on walking. I have to get out of here, distance myself from the crazy, explosive emotions she evoked. They're obviously some twisted mental metaphor for my final tumble off the deep end.

I'M GOING to try to avoid looking Nara's way from now on. Yesterday freaked me out. I'm obviously obsessing, and the only way to alleviate an obsession is to stay away from it. The problem is...I finally got my wish. I dreamed about her last night. And I woke this morning feeling the most rested I have in a very long time.

Not good.

How do you stop thinking about someone when their very presence makes you a better person? I *want* to get to know her. I want to know what music she likes, if she likes pizza as much as I do, why she volunteers at the shelter, if she's as smart to talk to about life stuff as she is in class, and I *really* want to know how she can do what she does.

Even though I'm not a part of her life, I console myself with the knowledge no one else seems to know about Nara's talent. I can't help how much I like being the only one. I ignore the fact she didn't share this with me. And, yes, I'm fully aware I delude myself on a daily basis. Makes getting through the day a lot easier.

I make it through a week and a half without gazing Nara's way. The only reason I'm able to manage this feat is because I've dreamed about her almost every night. Long, vivid dreams. It's like I finally did something right and the cosmos has rewarded me. I might not be part of Nara's real world, but at least she stars in my dream one. I tune out everything and everyone at school, even the lectures, so I don't break whatever magic spell has happened. I'm even able to mostly tune out Gravelly Voice when he shows up. I only cave a couple of times when I purposefully pass close to Nara in the hall, but I make sure never to look in her direction.

Eventually, I reach my breaking point. Dreams are like eating air and we all need sustenance to survive. The more I see Nara in my dreams, the more it makes me question why I can't try to get to know her. I haven't had any more crazy instances in my life. Daytime is mostly manageable now.

I'm sitting in History class when I make the decision to finally tune into my waking environment. As I listen to the lecture, I tilt my head and stare at the teacher. He's going over upcoming test stuff, repeating himself, apparently. I zone out and hold my breath as I finally slide my attention to Nara.

I slowly skim my gaze over her gorgeous face and infectious smile. Her green eyes are animated as she turns to hand the stack of papers to the guy behind her. She's so beautiful and yet she seems to have no idea just how much. My heart speeds up and then aches at the thought of just talking to her about random stuff like class assignments or soccer. The idea that she might reject my offer of friendship shuts down any thoughts of trying to speak to her. What if by trying to talk to her I stop dreaming about her? I think I might actually lose it if that happens. Setting my jaw, I glance back down at my sketchpad and start a new drawing, tuning everything out once more.

You can only shut off reality for so long before everything

begins to catch up with you. The only routine I've consistently kept up is to stop by the cemetery each morning. My gut tells me I'll see one of Marcus' toy cars waiting for me one day soon. Unfortunately, my grades are beginning to slide, so I grudgingly, little by little, start to tune into the rest of the real world, which is probablyfor the best. Gravelly Voice has been nonstop all morning, grating on my last nerve.

*Why do you think you can shut me off? Unlike everyone else, I'll always be your constant companion. Just stop trying to understand me. Drawing is pointless. Digging leads nowhere. I am darkness. Always here. Always with you. You can never make me go aw—*

My gaze strays to Nara and I smile and think, "Yes, I can."

She's the bright light shining in my periphery, edging out the creeping darkness. I can't help but stare directly into her brilliance. I'm all-in now, and as I continue to watch Nara interacting with classmates, the realization hits me so hard I freeze in complete surprise. How did *I* not see this before now?

*Because you wanted to believe you'd done something right to deserve having Nara all to yourself. This is what happens when you live in a dream world. And what are you going to do with this new information, Ethan?*

Nothing, I answer my own question as I walk out to my car at the end of the day.

*You're still not going to talk to her?*

What good will it do? The possibility of rejection and losing her forever is highly motivating to stay away.

*Remember Buddy?*

Shut up! I mentally bark. And now I'm arguing with myself. I'm so screwed up.

∽

I AWAKE SHAKING and gulping to breathe. Awareness sizzles through me as I take another jagged breath and am finally able to fill my lungs. I blink into the early morning darkness and jam shaking hands through my damp hair. Just when I think I've gotten control of my emotions, goose bumps scatter across my heated skin and a sense of wrongness rushes through me in intense vibrations.

*Nara!*

I need to get to school. I jerk upright and run for the bathroom.

I'm pretty sure I broke every speeding record getting to school, but with the blue and red lights flashing all around the building, the police are otherwise occupied.

I plug my earbuds in and jam my hands into my jeans, telling myself I'm just here to make sure Nara's okay. That my radar's off and she's fine. I make it as close to the school as the police will allow, but I don't see Nara anywhere. Then I see her walking across the parking lot in her ever-present dark sunglasses, heading for the school.

I turn away from the school and exhale a huge sigh of relief, telling my heart to stop its frantic pounding. I want so badly to talk to her, but the words lodge in my throat as I get closer. The thought of being shut down is enough to keep me staring straight ahead. I honestly don't think I could handle the rejection.

When I see her hand move toward me as we start to pass each other, I flinch in surprise and look her way. The brief press of her lips before her gaze reaches my face is the last thing I ever expected to see.

Even behind her shades, the moment Nara's eyes lock with mine is indescribable. I feel the rushing heat of her stare and think about dreams being nothing but air—and realize that to have her look at me like this and really see me is true sustenance.

She's sweetness sitting on the tip of my tongue, waiting for me to swallow.

My mouth starts to water.

Hell yeah, she's worth the risk of rejection. A thousand times worth it.

I swallow deeply and mumble, "Sorry," then pull my earbuds out. "What did you say?"

A brief smile touches her lips. "What's happening?"

Reality *always* trumps dreams. I hold her gaze and answer, "Bomb threat."

### Thank you for joining Ethan and Nara's journey!

IF YOU FOUND ETHAN an entertaining and enjoyable read, I hope you'll consider taking the time to leave a review and share your thoughts in the online bookstore where you purchased it. Your review could be the one to help another reader decide to read Ethan's story!

I hope you'll check out the rest of the books in the BRIGHTEST KIND OF DARKNESS series! Start with **BRIGHTEST KIND OF DARKNESS**. To keep up to date on when the next P.T. Michelle book will release, join my free newsletter http://bit.ly/11tqAQN

If you haven't read **BRIGHTEST KIND OF DARK-NESS** yet, turn the page for an excerpt from book one where it all begins!

# BRIGHTEST KIND OF DARKNESS
## (BOOK 1) - EXCERPT

Once we'd stowed my stuff in the back of my car, Ethan opened the car door and waited for me to get in. Even though I wanted to ask him so many questions, I was afraid to speak. It felt like we'd moved to a whole new level in our friendship, but I wasn't sure what that level was.

Every nerve ending urged me to hug him, to show my appreciation, but I was unsure. Would he pull away? I didn't need any more rejection in my life. "Thank you for being there," I said in an unsteady voice.

Ethan clasped my wrist and pulled me into his arms, holding me close. "I'll always be here for you."

I shuddered against his chest, mumbling into his flannel shirt. "You weren't at school and I didn't see you after practice. I thought for sure no one would hear me scream when those guys finally got their hands on—"

Warm fingers tilted my chin up. "I had something to do today, but I'd never leave you hanging. When I saw your stuff on the field and then I heard a guy yelling, 'She went this way,' in the woods..." He paused, tensing. "I freaked."

"You got to me just in time." I tried to smile but my lips trembled. "Who knew knights wore flannel shirts and Led Zeppelin tees?" I knew I sounded like a goof, but I didn't care. I wanted him to know how much his rescue meant to me.

Ethan leaned close and I closed my eyes as he lightly kissed my cheekbone, then my forehead. He had no idea that his gentle kiss had melted something inside me, how much I craved the physical connection. His warm lips lingered against my skin for a second before he took a step back and shoved his hands in his jeans pockets.

"I'm no hero, Nara." His gaze narrowed briefly toward the woods. "Go home. I'll see you tomorrow."

Get **BRIGHTEST KIND OF DARKNESS** now!

**Bad in Boots series
(Contemporary Romance, 18+)**
Harm's Hunger
Ty's Temptation
Colt's Choice
Josh's Justice

**Kendrian Vampires series
(Paranormal Romance, 18+)**
A Taste for Passion
A Taste for Revenge
A Taste for Control

**Stay up-to-date on her latest releases:**

**Join P.T's Newsletter:**
http://bit.ly/11tqAQN

**Visit P.T. :**
**Website:** http://www.ptmichelle.com
**Twitter:** https://twitter.com/PT_Michelle
**Facebook:** https://www.facebook.com/PTMichelleAuthor
**Instagram:** http://instagram.com/p.t.michelle
**Goodreads:**
http://www.goodreads.com/author/show/4862274.P_T_Mi
chelle

**P.T. Michelle's Facebook Readers' Group:**
https://www.facebook.com/groups/PTMichelleReadersGro
up/

# BRIGHTEST KIND OF DARKNESS SERIES BONUS MATERIAL

The bonus scenes that follow fall at different points in the Brightest Kind of Darkness series.

## ** SPOILER WARNING: DON'T READ ANY OF THESE UNTIL YOU'VE READ THE SERIES.**

You're still here, reading, huh? For those like you who just can't wait, I've labeled the top of each excerpt/deleted scene to let you know where it falls in the order of the series, so that you can read it in the correct order without spoiling your enjoyment of the books.

# CHAPTER 22 FROM BKOD FROM ETHAN'S POINT-OF-VIEW

## A BRIGHTEST KIND OF DARKNESS SERIES EXTRA

**\*\* SPOILER WARNING \*\***
**READ AFTER YOU'VE READ BRIGHTEST KIND**
**OF DARKNESS, BOOK 1**

*I* pulled into Nara's driveway early and cut the engine. She wasn't due back from practice for another fifteen minutes or so. *Would she believe me?* I shrugged off the tension in my shoulders and glanced at my spiral notebook sitting in the passenger seat. I'd brought my drawings, hoping they would convince her that Fate could be seen.

My fingers thrummed on the dash as time ticked by. I wasn't sure we could make my idea work, but if Nara wore that crystal necklace that had allowed her to see my dreams while we combined our dream powers, that just might be enough for her to see Fate. Then she could face him.

Why couldn't I face Fate for her? I felt powerless, inept in the one thing that mattered to me, protecting Nara. I'd never despised anyone as much as I hated this skulking invisible entity! I gripped the steering wheel as red flashed in my eyes. Something cracked and I grimaced as I uncurled my fingers. A new split ran along the curved black edge. Shit.

Jamming my fingers into my hair, I gripped my bangs at the thought of the monsters Nara would come face-to-face with in my nightmares in order for her to face Fate in her own dreams. I tasted blood and realized I'd bitten my cheek. I wish there was another way, but I couldn't think of any. Fate's attacks on Nara had escalated. Between Nara's stubborn heart and her need to help others, she only made him angrier.

I couldn't lose her. I'd do anything, beat the shit out of Fate if I could, break the law...whatever it took to keep her safe. Screw Fate! Rage built within me so swiftly my hands began to shake. Curling my hands into fists didn't help. I took several deep breaths and tried to regain control, but it felt as if the darkness that coiled inside me embraced this anger, welcomed it even.

With a flick of my wrist, I flipped the sun visor down to stare at the drawings I'd pinned there. A picture of Nara furrowing her brow as she wrote something on her palm in class, another of her laughing in the hall while she dribbled a soccer ball, another sketch was of her scrunching her nose while she pretended to study. I'd drawn each of these before we'd met, before Nara had ever said a word to me. Mesmerized by her smile and the spark in her gorgeous eyes, I'd watched her. Every day. I'd been intrigued by her confidence. Even now I sometimes felt unworthy that she's with me. I've loved every smile she's turned my way, cherished each one.

My fingers shook as I traced them over her features, careful not to smear a single line. She always calmed me. Because of Nara, I looked more deeply at people, when all I used to see and feel was negative stuff. Focusing on her smile helped me regain control of myself. I needed to be calm and confident when I showed her these drawings and told her my plan.

A sudden buzzing rippled across my skin, the sensation washing through me in vibrating waves of increasing heat. My chest tightened and fear clogged my lungs. I'd felt a similar vibe before when Fate had attacked Nara. I fired up the engine and jammed the stick shift in reverse. My tires squealed as I tore out of her neighborhood.

The speedometer hit ninety by the time I got to school. I screeched into the soccer fields parking lot, then skidded to a stop next to Nara's car.

I frowned when I scanned the field and didn't immediately see Nara. Where is she? Then my gaze landed on the overturned goal and Nara was pinned under it. *Nara!*

I don't remember getting out of my car or running to the goal. My gaze stayed locked on Nara's limp form as I prayed for the first time in my life. *Please God, let her be okay. Please!*

It felt like my heart had been cinched in a vise when I saw her staring sightlessly into the night sky, icy rain drizzling on her slack features. My fingers dug into the goal post and suddenly my heart pumped so hard and so fast I wondered if it had doubled in size. The goal thronged as it landed, completely flipped over in the opposite direction.

My legs gave out and I fell to my knees beside Nara, touching her throat. No pulse fluttered under my fingers. "No, Nara! God no!" I rocked back on my heels and screamed to the sky, furious with God for trying to take her from me.

*Be calm. Use your knowledge to save her.* Words echoed inside my head as if another part of me, my rational self, had taken over.

I fisted my hands on my thighs, took three deep breaths,

then told myself the steps for CPR over and over in my head until my hands began to move on their own over her chest, pumping in quick bursts. Tilting her head back, I held her nose, then breathed life back into her, focusing on my task. *Breathe Nara! Breathe for me.* Anger overwhelmed my fear. I welcomed the white-hot emotion. Anger I could handle. I began to push on her chest again, gritting out, "Don't you die on me!"

A cool tingling ran along my arm, and I almost paused it was so surreal, but I couldn't stop my task. I had to jump start Nara's heart, keep her breathing until she could do so on her own.

But as I moved through the repetitive CPR motions with no response from Nara, and my worry began to shift to near paralyzing panic, something kept buzzing in my ear, a nagging sound I couldn't ignore.

I slid my attention to the noise on my right and blinked at the strange flock of ravens flying in what appeared to be haphazard chaos. As I stared at the birds, I saw a kind of pattern appear as they moved toward me. Their chaos wasn't chaos at all, but an organized outline that formed around something I couldn't see. They were trying to show me that whatever it was…it was coming. And fast.

My skin buzzed as if electrified, and suddenly I felt as if my space was being invaded. Whatever it was…I sensed its cold presence, the finality of it, slam down my spine as if a spike of ice had been sledge-hammered through my skull.

Somehow I knew it was here for Nara. To take her from me forever.

*No! She's mine!*

The rage I experienced earlier when I thought of Fate messing with Nara felt like tepid bathwater compared to the lava-flow of fury that wailed like an erupting volcano in my body. As molten heat boiled through my veins, that logical, reasoned half of me took over with fierce, directed vengeance. My hands lifted and my palms flicked toward the invisible intruder as I spoke from the darkest place inside me. "You can't have her!"

A surge shifted with the direction of my anger. Hot lava shot through my veins, flowing along my fingers in waves. Power erupted from me so forcefully, the vacuum-pull tugged on my entire body.

When the birds flew back, "What the hell just happened?" shot through my mind, but I didn't have time to think about it. The ravens had already recovered and were moving back toward us at a much faster pace than before. Whatever it was, I'd pissed it off, but I didn't give a shit. My attention shifted to Nara as I pressed on her chest again with focused determination. *Wake, up, damn it. I love you! I need the chance to tell you that, to tell you how much you mean to me.*

She lay there unmoving, staring at nothing. The thought I'd never see her smile again, feel her lips on mine, her hands touching my face, tore at my heart. "You can't be gone, Nara!"

Warm tears flowed down my face, the salt mixing with the patter of rain hitting my lips. "Don't leave me!" *Losing you will break me.* Tilting her neck, I whispered against her lips, "I love you," then pressed my mouth to hers, breathing every ounce of my will, my own life into her.

Nara coughed, fluttering her eyelids and my heart leapt. "Nara? Thank God!" I touched her cheek, the ache in my chest releasing in relief. "Can you hear me? Say something? How do you feel?"

When she placed a cold hand over mine and rasped, "Thank you," my love for her rolled along my body in a thankful shudder. *No, Sunshine.* Thank you *for coming back to me. I'll never let you go. Ever.*

Kissing her forehead, I lifted her into my arms. As I gripped her close and talked about taking her to the hospital, my heart made its own promise. *It's time to tell you how I feel.*

# UNFORESEEN

## A BRIGHTEST KIND OF DARKNESS SERIES EXTRA

**\*\* SPOILER WARNING \*\***
**READ BRIGHTEST KIND OF DARKNESS (BOOK1 )**
**AND LUCID (BOOK 2) BEFORE READING THIS**

The palm-leaved ceiling fan turned in a slow, rhythmic thrum, stirring the sticky summer heat. Humidity thickened the tension surrounding the dark-haired man, causing perspiration to slide along the worry lines in his face as he sat down in the straight-backed chair.

Crawling into the man's lap, the little blonde girl watched their serene host walk around the coffee table and sit down on the floral patterned couch across from them. When the child continued to stare in awe at the crystal beads decorating her long dark braids, the woman smiled and lifted her hair, holding the ends up so the sunlight caught the crystals. Rainbow colored lights danced on the girl's pink shirt. With a giggle of delight, she tried to catch the rainbow dots on her chest and belly.

"Invisible fireflies," the woman whispered with a conspiratorial wink before she released her braids and began to shuffle a stack of oversized cards on the coffee table's polished surface, her movements smooth and assured.

The little girl clapped her hands, her green eyes flicking to the man. "Are we playing a game, Daddy?"

"Kind of." He kissed the back of her head, then set the five-year-old on her feet as he addressed the woman. "Things have happened…" Concern edged his words as he briefly touched the small white bandage on his daughter's forehead. "Things I can't explain. My sister hoped you might have insight."

With a nod of understanding, the woman fanned out the shuffled cards face down toward him. "Take two cards."

He took two cards and turned them face up at the woman's request.

The man and woman exchanged glances. "Can you try once more?" he asked, tension making him sound hoarse.

She pressed her lips together, but reshuffled the cards, then held them out to him.

He stared at the cards and flexed his jaw. Sliding his gaze sideways, he spoke to the little girl, "Why don't you pick them, sweetheart?"

"Ooh, a different game!" Squealing with excitement, she sang "Eeny, meeny, miney, moe" twice, one for each card she picked, and then turned them over on the table like she'd seen him do.

"Having the child choose them makes no difference," their host said with a sigh, tapping the two cards. "They're always the same: The Wheel of Fortune and Justice cards speak of unforeseen changes and destiny."

After she laid down several more cards in a specific pattern, the woman's face crinkled in concentration. A few seconds later, her deep brown gaze shifted nervously to the little girl, who'd lost interest in the game and was squatting to pet the orange tabby cat rubbing against the coffee table leg. "This doesn't bode well for her."

They spoke in low tones, and then the man picked up the child, gathering her little body close. She hugged his neck and patted his cheeks. "Is it time to go?"

He nodded and smiled, forcing a light tone. "Let's go get that ice cream I promised you, Nari."

# DESTINY DELETED SCENE

## A BRIGHTEST KIND OF DARKNESS SERIES EXTRA

## ** SPOILER WARNING **
## READ THIS AFTER YOU'VE READ: ETHAN, BRIGHTEST KIND OF DARKNESS, LUCID, AND DESTINY

*S*cenes are deleted from books for many reasons. Sometimes it's for word count. Sometimes it's because the scene doesn't move the story forward. No matter HOW good a scene it is, if it doesn't do that, then it goes on the cutting room floor. In the case of this scene from DESTINY, I was running very high on word count and needed to take it down. This scene is 2K, so half a chapter!

The information that was learned in this cut scene had to be moved to another part of the book, and if you've read DESTINY, you'll remember exactly where I weaved in the new information.

As a point of reference to where this scene fit into the story, in the original draft of DESTINY...this scene is the night Nara went to the Mindblown club with Lainey and friends. It takes place later in the evening after Nara had seen Ethan at the cemetery and told him there are two types of demons–Inferni and Furiae–and exactly how Furiae are created.

## Exclusive Deleted Scene From Destiny

"EARTH TO NARA," Drystan calls above the hip-hop music blaring all around us. "You coming?"

My mind is still on my aunt's hushed words as she hugged me before she left: "Dinner was…interesting. Thank your mom again for inviting me at the last minute. Mr. Dixon seems to make her happy and I'm thrilled to have finally met your infamous Gran. I do believe I've found a kindred soul. I might have to go visit her and her friend Clara once she's feeling better. Their friendly rivalry is hilarious!"

Pulling back, she'd cupped my cheeks and smiled. "I can see the guilt in your face, Inara. Don't feel that way. I think it's for the best that we don't tell your mom about my brother right now." Her eyes welled with tears and she quickly sniffed them back. "We may never find him. Why bring a new kind of pain into your mom's heart?"

She paused and glanced upstairs toward my room where I'd quickly stashed the box she handed me under my bed while mom was introducing Mr. Dixon to Gran. "Open that when you're alone. It's all dry-cleaned and ready to go for you. If your mom asks where you got it, just say you picked it up at a retro store at the mall."

Drystan's tug on my arm yanks me back to the present. I follow him into the dark nightclub with its sparkling starry-night walls, past the bar and café tables surrounded by college-aged people drinking and laughing.

I guess I'd zoned out pretty hard, because Lainey, Matt, and a couple of girl friends of Drystan's, Maddie and Megan, who met us there are already dancing in the throng of people on the floating dance floor. It actually doesn't float, but the swirling shades of blue that make a water pattern in the glossy plastic beneath your feet can make you feel woozy if you look down too long. I keep my eyes on Drystan's back so I don't get dizzy.

Once we reach our group, Drystan announces, "Blitzed girl is now found. Mission accomplished."

"I'm not blitzed." I scowl at him. "I'm completely sober."

"Well, you were somewhere *not* here," Drystan says in a dry tone right before Maddie and Megan stop grinding against each other long enough to pull him between them.

"Get a room already," Lainey calls out to them, then untangles herself from Matt's hold to hook her arm around my neck. Before I can say a word, she jerks me forward and plants a big fat kiss on my lips.

"What the heck was that?" I sputter, pushing away, wide-eyed.

"Hell yeah!" Matt yells, a huge grin on his face.

Lainey blows him a kiss, then slides her gaze back to me. "Just wanting to make sure you're really here with us now. Is Ethan coming? Were you texting him or something? Drystan swore you were buying a drink."

I stiffen my spine. "I'm here! And I doubt Ethan can come tonight. He has some stuff he needs to do."

"What'd I miss?" Drystan leans in, his gaze darting to Matt.

While Matt fills him in on our girl-on-girl kiss, Lainey looks me up and down. "Really, Nara? You're *still* not dancing."

As Drystan's gaze jerks from Matt to me, my hips start to

move and I raise my hands over my head, snapping my fingers. "Happy?"

"Immensely!" Lainey says, wrapping her arms back around her boyfriend's neck.

The music changes from a slower beat to a much faster one, and my hips began to move on their own. Lainey's right. I haven't allowed myself to have fun lately. As the heavy bass sound pulses through me, I close my eyes and let myself go, moving with the music.

I hear Lainey's laugh just a foot away from me, right before she clasps my hips and begins to dance close behind me.

If Lainey wants to give Matt a show, he's definitely going to get one. I move my hips in a figure eight swivel, then bend my knees, lowering myself down toward the floor and then up, making it hard for her to match my moves. Somehow she keeps up. I feel her thighs moving behind mine, pressing close.

One of the girls giggles, then slides in front of me. As she gyrates and her breasts lightly brush against my chest, I hear Matt say, "Daayum, I want some of that action."

I pretend not to hear him and start to press closer to the girl in front of me, but I'm yanked back flush against Lainey at the same time Drystan says next to my ear, "'ell no! I'm not sharing with anyone. She's all mine."

"Drystan!" I quickly stiffen and turn to face him.

While Lainey, Matt, and the girls laugh at their joke they'd played before they pair off dancing once more, Drystan raises his hands innocently. "What?"

I glance over at Maddie and Megan, who've moved on to dance with a couple other random guys. I see their blonde and brunette heads swaying to the music as they wave their arms into the cloud of dry ice smoke that's now floating through the air above us. I laugh and shake my head. "Guess it's a free for all tonight, huh?"

Drystan smiles and begins to move to the song. As he edges closer to the girls, he nods to my suddenly still body. "Come on, Nara. It's just about having fun."

Giggling, I start to raise my arms and swing my hips, but someone clasps my wrist. I'm tugged through a huge group of people and away from my friends.

It's too crowded and smoky to see who's playing some new joke on me, so I start to pull hard and struggle to free myself from the viselike hold on my arm. "Let me go!"

I'm now at the edge of the dance floor where there's less smoke and Ethan looms over me. "I came to talk to you, to tell you I spoke to Danielle. The last thing I expected to see was that Welsh bastard's hands all over you."

"I thought that was Lainey behind me, Ethan."

Ethan's scowl loses some of its bite. "You were getting it on with your best friend?"

I roll my eyes. "It was meant to be a joke."

Anger eases from his expression, but then his eyes narrow. "You might've thought it was a joke, but you didn't see his face. He was into it, Nara. If his hands moved any closer to your ass or chest, that guy would be eating the floor."

I glance over my shoulder as the fast moving song segues into a slow, sexy beat, full of want and angst. Through the haze of smoke, Maddie and Megan have draped themselves on Drystan's front and back like cheap fur coats, while his hands expertly pet and rub all over their faux pelts. "Um, yeah. He's *so* into me."

Ethan's gaze zeros in on Drystan. "He's a guy. They take advantage of any situation."

My head whips back to him. "Did you take advantage of your situation?"

His brow crinkles. "What situation?"

My insides tighten, but I finally bring up the issue that's been on my mind since I learned Danielle wasn't his cousin. "You were alone with Danielle for nearly a month."

The dark storm that swells in Ethan's eyes makes me take a step back, but his hold on my arm keeps me from putting too much space between us.

"I thought I was pretty clear how I feel about you last night," he says as he reaches up and folds his other hand along the back of my neck. Fingers flexing, his warmth seeps into my skin as he tugs me forward until my chest is flush with his. "But I guess I'll just have to show you all over again."

"That's not an answer," I breathe out in a hushed voice. His solid strength and arousing masculine smell are making my body hum to life despite my efforts to remain unaffected.

"When it comes to you, actions seem far more impactful." Ethan wraps an arm around my waist and starts to move his hips to the seductive rhythm of the song.

I had no idea he could dance like this, but I like seeing another side to him. I match his sensual movements beat for beat, our hips moving with each other as if tethered together.

A sexy smile touches his lips as he slides his fingers into my hair. Tracing his thumb along my jaw, he applies slight pressure behind my ear and tilts my head down. As my forehead touches his chest and all I can see is our hips moving together, he whispers huskily next to my ear, "We have perfect rhythm, Sunshine."

My pulse races as his lips slide along my jaw toward my mouth. The brush of our bodies moving to the song's beat and Ethan making me watch us move together amps my desire to feel him pressing against me intimately once more. It's what I want, but not what I need right now. I jerk my head up and blink away thoughts of us together. "You came here to tell me something."

"It can wait. I told you, *we're* just as important."

"If it's about Danielle—"

Ethan's mouth captures mine in a slow, heart-stopping kiss.

When he cups my jaw, I open my lips under his, welcoming the feel of his tongue sliding against mine. As soon as I press against him, Ethan's hold on me tightens and his hand glides to my hip, pulling me flush to his muscular frame.

My body tingles and my thighs shake when his hardness brushes against me with our movements. I clutch his jeans' belt loops and twist the denim tight to keep from collapsing in his arms.

Ethan kisses my temple, then says gruffly in my ear as we slowly spin to the song, "Did you know that I drew pictures of you way before I met you?"

I glance up at him and shake my head.

"Or that I pretended to be an angel named Protection and Vengeance to protect you from some douchebag at school intent on making you his next sexual conquest?"

"Protection and Vengeance?" I stop dancing and blink past the moisture in my eyes, totally surprised and flattered. "No, I didn't."

He brushes away the lone tear that trickles down my cheek. "I'm not telling you this to make me look better in your eyes. I'm telling you so you know that you've been important to me for longer than you realize."

I exhale slowly and smile. "I know we've been through a lot. And everything that's going on right now is putting stress on our relationship—"

"Ethan!" a woman's voice calls out, drawing our attention

Danielle's standing near the bar area wearing all black again. From her tall, shiny boots, to her slicked-back, severe ponytail, she has a look about her that makes me think she's going to pull a riding crop from her boot any second. She's all business.

"Come on," she mouths, waving for him.

Ethan exhales heavily. "We've got to check out some other places that demon told us about."

I sigh as I release him. "What did Danielle say about Furiae?"

"She said this Madeline person doesn't have her facts straight. We aren't creating Furiae."

"How does she know that for sure?"

His lips thin in a stubborn line. "She just does."

"*How*, Ethan?"

"Because she's—"

I want to choke him when he clamps his mouth shut. "She's what?"

Ethan shakes his head. "Trust me, Nara. She just knows."

"Ethan." Danielle's standing a few feet away from us now on the main level, her arms folded. "This is prime time. We need to go now."

Ethan kisses my forehead, then hops down from the dance floor. Glancing up at me, he says, "I'll call you tomorrow."

As I watch Ethan and Danielle head toward the entrance of the club, Drystan's voice drifts over the music behind me. "What the 'ell is their deal? Now he's showing her around nightclubs? Friends don't let friends do the doormat dance, Nara."

"Shut up, coatrack," I snap before I walk away to find Lainey.

## ACKNOWLEDGEMENTS

To my critique partner, Trisha Wolfe, thank you for helping make *Ethan* the best it can be.

To my beta readers: Dani Snell, Heather Potts, and Allison Konop, thank you for your amazing support of the Brightest Kind of Darkness series, for your valuable input, and for being the first to stamp your avid approval on *Ethan*!

To my husband, thank you for being so proud and telling everyone to check out my books.

And to my children, who're always willing to give their opinions on covers and such. See, Mom does listen! Thank you for your support and patience, and for understanding that when I'm working on a book and say I'll be there in a minute, you should probably start prepping dinner. All my efforts to make sure you don't solely live on noodles and hotdogs when you go on to college is totally paying off. :)

# ABOUT THE AUTHOR

P.T. Michelle is the *NEW YORK TIMES, USA TODAY*, and international bestselling author of the New Adult contemporary romance series IN THE SHADOWS, the YA/New Adult crossover series BRIGHTEST KIND OF DARKNESS, and the romance series: BAD IN BOOTS, KENDRIAN VAMPIRES and SCIONS (listed under Patrice Michelle). She keeps a spiral notepad with her at all times, even on her nightstand. When P.T. isn't writing, she can usually be found reading or taking pictures of landscapes, sunsets and anything beautiful or odd in nature.

To learn when the next P.T. Michelle book will release, join her free newsletter http://bit.ly/11tqAQN

*Follow P.T. Michelle*
www.ptmichelle.com

facebook.com/PTMichelleAuthor

twitter.com/PT_Michelle

instagram.com/p.t.michelle

youtube.com/PTMichelleAuthor

Printed in Great Britain
by Amazon

75344896R00069